Mistletoe and Murder

by
Evelyn James

A Clara Fitzgerald Mystery
Book 5

Red Raven Publications

Cover images from Stock Xchng and Wikimedia

Other Books in
The Clara Fitzgerald Series

Chapter One

Clara Fitzgerald, Brighton's first female private detective, had firm views on the paranormal. Namely that it was all hogwash. Only once in her career as a detective had she been asked to investigate the supernatural, and that was under great duress. How any rational person could believe in ghosts defied Clara's imagination and she made a point of avoiding cases with even a hint of the supernatural about them. She had not, for instance, accepted the case of the husband who believed his wife's ghost had returned to tell him that her correct will was not the one read out after her funeral. Naturally enough, the woman's real last will (according to the widower) left everything to her husband and cut out the rest of her family. The husband wanted an 'unbiased observer' to help him find the real will as referred to by the ghost. Clara suspected either delusion or fraud and wisely declined.

On more than one instance Clara had been contacted due to the mistaken belief that she was a private detective not just for the living, but also for the dead. She had been asked to investigate hauntings and the post-mortem claims of deceased relatives. Clara had politely pointed such letter writers in the direction of those better equipped to deal with such matters, namely the Society for Psychical Research (Brighton Division). So when the letter came from London, her first instinct was to turn it down, but the more Clara read, the more intrigued she became and the more she felt that here was a real case with flesh and blood suspects and, of course, living victims.

The letter came on a drizzly afternoon a week before Christmas. Snow was threatening in the air. Annie, the Fitzgeralds' industrious maid, had lain in enough supplies for a siege, let alone a bout of bad weather. In between feeding the enormous Christmas cake she had prepared with whisky, she was keeping her eye on the butcher who had promised her the finest goose he could obtain (but whom she suspected of saying exactly the same thing to every lady who entered his shop). Tommy Fitzgerald, Clara's brother, had a cold and was snuffling his way through A Christmas Carol by Dickens as he sat wrapped in blankets and a scarf by the roaring fire in the parlour. He had said more than once that morning that he was convinced he was dying, and that this was the worst cold he had ever had. Clara had retreated to the garden room after his moans of self-pity had tormented her for over an hour and was working through her post. She was a neglectful correspondent and often forgot to read her letters for several days – until they formed a towering pile on the hall stand that was impossible to ignore.

That was how, amidst the gas bill and a pamphlet for spring bulbs, she found the letter from Miss Sampford and her curiosity was peaked.

Dear Miss Clara Fitzgerald,

Your name was passed to me through a friend in Brighton who highly commended your abilities. I require your assistance on a very confusing matter and I dare say you will call me foolish, but please read this whole letter before discarding my request. My friend recommended you, for your rational and down-to-earth thinking, which sounds very much like the sort of person I need right about now.

Let me explain myself a little further. I am a spinster of 81 years living on my own, very sufficient, means. For the last 10 years, since the death of my dear mother at the grand age of nearly 100, I have lived in Berkeley Square, London with a small household of staff. I have been very happy here and I had hoped to end my days in this little portion of the world. Unfortunately I feel that may now be denied me.

I am suffering the torments of a ghost. Now, I hope you have not thrown this letter down with disgust, please let me explain. I am a rational, modern individual and therefore I find myself very hard-pressed to believe in the existence of malicious spirits, yet the evidence of my own eyes has led me to fear this is the very case. Over the last six months strange occurrences have been reported in my house by everyone from servants to friends and neighbours. Five maids have simply up and left, refusing to stay in this house, now my cook who has been with me these last 24 years is threatening to go to unless the matter is resolved. I was inclined to discredit the notion myself, until I saw a figure hovering over my bed one night. I feared a burglar and hastily rang the bell, but almost at once the figure was gone and I was alone again. Since then I have heard noises, seen shadows and in general felt very uncomfortable in my own home.

My nephew resides with me when he is in town and has suggested we call in the Spiritualists, in fact, he is all for a massive ghost hunt, which gives me quite a thrill of horror being such a private person. However, something must be done. I fear I have become overwhelmed by it all and cannot view the matter clearly. I need a rational, dare I say, cynical mind to examine this matter with fresh eyes. While my senses see and hear things I cannot believe real, my thoughts still run to the possibility of a hoax being perpetrated on myself. For what reason, you ask? And for this I offer two suggestions.

1) A certain gentleman has expressed a desire to buy my house and has been pestering me on the matter for the last twelve-month. He has been most insistent and, quite honestly,

has become a nuisance. It occurs to me he may have manufactured a ghost to make it untenable for me to remain in my home.

2) I mentioned my nephew Elijah resides here and while I do not perceive any malice in him personally, I am aware that some of my extended family find my continual good health troublesome. For instance, my brother's son, William Henry, now runs the family estates and my yearly annuity comes from that same estate, as arranged by my dear late father and intended to support me for all my years. From what little I have heard I suspect the estate finances are not as abundant as once thought and my small annuity is seen as a drain on them further. My £500 per annum could no doubt be better used, in William Henry's opinion, to sustain his own family. I have, therefore, come to wonder whether someone would be inclined to try and scare me to death, as a means of being rid of me. I am no legal mind, but I assume this would still be deemed murder?

As you see there may be a very logical and completely corporeal reason for this ghost and for that I need you to investigate.

I do hope you have read this far and now I must ask a rather awkward question. I feel there is a need for urgency and I would much appreciate it if you would come down and stay with me over the festive period. I ask this firstly because the manifestations I have described have recently grown more disturbing and secondly because most of my family will be in London for Christmas and several will be staying with me, giving you a prime opportunity to investigate them. And lastly because my nephew has arranged for a rather obnoxious ghost hunter to come down over Christmas, and I am really not sure I can stand all this talk of spooks and spectres without another rational and sympathetic human being to talk to.

Please do come for Christmas, I beg you. I apologise for my desperation, but I really begin to feel fearful for my life. Bring whomever you desire, I can surely accommodate them and it is the least consideration I can offer for my sudden disruption of

your Christmas plans. If you could respond as soon as possible I
would be most grateful.
    Yours Sincerely
    Miss Edith Sampford

Clara glanced at the postmark on the letter; it was dated two days ago. She cursed herself for not opening her post sooner. Clara did not for one moment believe a ghost had taken up residence in Miss Sampford's home, but she did sense something was off in the household. Perhaps it was just someone making mischief, but could she ignore Miss Sampford's fears that much worse was afoot? Clearly the poor woman was very frightened and feeling distinctly alone in her troubles; that in itself might make her more susceptible to murderous fears, but could Clara really dismiss her concerns so lightly? She mused on the matter for a while longer, watching the dull clouds drift across a bleak sky.

Of course, Annie had made plans for Christmas and Oliver Bankes, the local photographer, had been asked for Christmas dinner. But the cake and vegetables would last until New Year's and surely any good ghost hunter (especially the sceptical sort) had a photographer in their arsenal of 'expert helpers' these days? Christmas in London could be quite jolly, the Capital was bound to be buzzing with shoppers, amusements and other festivities. Clara had always fancied doing her Christmas shopping in Harrods, perhaps now was that opportunity? In any case, a cry for help had been issued and Clara did not turn down genuine cries for help.

She rose from her chair and went to find Tommy.

"What are your views on ghosts?" She asked the snuffling invalid.

Tommy peered up from reddened eyes.

"You know them already. I think spirits are a distinct possibility."

"And I don't, so that makes a perfect partnership. How do you fancy Christmas in London?"

Tommy looked baffled, trying to take in this sudden change of subject.

"London?"

"A plea for help has come for me from the Capital. An elderly lady in distress who is being tormented by a supposed haunting, but which could equally be a malicious hoax. She has requested my presence at once."

"Over Christmas?"

"Yes."

Tommy blew his nose into a handkerchief.

"And you want me to come?"

"You, Annie, Oliver Bankes too. We'll make a regular party of it, and you will all have your roles to play. Annie will be our eyes and ears in the servants' quarters, Oliver will use his knowledge of photography to get evidence that our ghost is very much a living person and you, as always, will be my first-class assistant and researcher."

"Cheers." Tommy sniffled.

"Well, what do you say?"

Tommy gave a long sigh that ended in a cough.

"I am assuming my other option is to stay home alone?"

"Your cold will be better in a day or two, and then you will enjoy yourself."

"Where exactly are we going?"

"Berkeley Square."

"Fine then." Tommy groaned, "I suppose I can die there as well as I can die here."

"No talk of dying around Miss Sampford, she is a very scared lady. I will speak with Annie and make the arrangements."

Clara bustled out before Tommy could make further comment. She found Annie next and explained the matter. There was a moment of petulance when Annie realised her Christmas cake, lovingly tended, would be neglected for a whole week or two, but Clara compromised by insisting she must bring it along, beautifully iced, to be shared by all at Berkeley Square. Annie was mostly mollified, admitting that she had always wondered what the kitchens were like in a posh London household. As for Oliver Bankes, his first disappointment at learning Clara was heading to London for Christmas was quickly overridden by his excitement to learn he could join her. He was even more elated when she explained how he was to act as a 'spirit photographer' and use all his tricks of the trade to capture the image of the ghost, which Clara had now convinced herself was a very inconsiderate person playing silly beggars. With everyone on-board, there was only one person left to contact. Fortunately Miss Sampford was on the telephone.

"Hello, is that Miss Sampford's residence?"

"Yes, Miss Sampford speaking." A strong, un-quavering voice replied. Miss Sampford did not sound like a frail old woman, nor did she sound in anyway foolish or prone to superstition.

"This is Clara Fitzgerald, I just received your letter..."

"Oh Miss Fitzgerald! I am so delighted to hear from you, I was growing concerned. Do say you accept my invitation to come London?"

There was the desperation so palpable in the letter.

"I would be delighted to accept the invitation and to rid you of your most inconsiderate house guest."

Miss Sampford gave a chuckle.

"It almost sounds as if you are talking about my nephew, poor dear boy. But I do understand you, will you come at once?"

"I shall have to make a few last arrangements, but I would expect to be with you tomorrow."

"That will be good, this blasted ghost hunter and his people are due to arrive tomorrow night and with all my worries I have dreaded facing them alone. The fellow states he is bringing a 'team' of investigators. What on earth can that mean? The only team we had in my day were those of the horse variety. Perhaps he intends to pull a carriage through my house!"

Clara found herself smiling, already warming to Miss Sampford.

"I will be there as soon as I can. I shall be bringing my brother, a family friend and my maid, if that is all right? The friend was a Christmas guest who I can hardly turn away."

"Yes, that is quite all right, I imagined as much since I requested you at such short notice. It is jolly good as it might mean turning out a few relatives to the nearest hotel. Doesn't that sound awful? I do feel fondly for some of my family, you know."

"I quite understand Miss Sampford."

"Then I shall let you get on. Goodbye Miss Fitzgerald, I do look forward to seeing you."

Clara put down the phone receiver and started a mental list of the things she must pack to ensure she was fully prepared for the case. Tommy gave a cry from the parlour;

"It just started snowing!"

Clara glanced up.

"Oh good! It will show up any footprints our ghost leaves behind!"

Chapter Two

London was still dusting itself off from four years of war and the subsequent financial downturn. All those soldiers coming home to a changed world, one where there was little work and even less money. One where women were demanding an equal place, along with the poor, the disabled and just about everyone else who felt penalised for being different. The Capital groaned at protests and riots, but then it had always done that. Ministers in parliament yelled at each other and made promises impossible to keep. The factories closed or expanded, depending as much on circumstances as on the wit of their owners. The rich got richer, the poor got poorer and, on the whole, the city rolled on as it had always done. Adapting, adjusting and surviving.

Brighton and London had developed a symbiotic relationship over the years; Brighton being the ideal holiday spot for the worn-out Londoner. The great and the good had gone to Brighton for the alleged health giving waters, following in the shadow of the Prince Regent who, most famously, built the fabulously eccentric Royal Pavilion – a mishmash of domes, gilt decoration and radiant tiles. During the years of the great steam revolution Brighton's popularity soared among the middle and working classes who now found it possible to make day-trips to the town. Brighton residents might argue that this, while boosting certain forms of economy, had rather lowered the 'tone'. Londoners of all ranks and kinds descended on the resort whenever they were able, including those of a criminal inclination. But whatever the downsides of being connected to the Capital via road and rail, it had plenty of upsides as well. Not least the ease with which Brightoners could visit the city.

Clara felt London was one of those places it was nice to visit, but not somewhere she would want to live. The number of vehicles on the road was a shock for a start and the terrible roar of the traffic, coupled with the yells of irate drivers, made her shudder. Within her first hour in the city she saw a motorcar skid and nearly collide with a horse-drawn milk cart. The driver of the motorcar emerged from his mechanical beast and began berating the fellow driving the cart for getting in his way. A heated argument began and embroiled several passers-by, in general on the side of the milkman. Clara watched it all from the relative safety of an omnibus, wondering how anyone could live all their days in such a madhouse of a place.

She had hoped that Berkeley Square, one of the more prestigious parts of London, would at least afford some peace from the craziness of the city – but she was completely wrong. While Berkeley Square had begun life as a classic collection of Georgian townhouses to accommodate the extremely wealthy (and the odd MP), the intervening years had seen many of its properties transformed into businesses and the Square thronged with shoppers, businessmen and traffic. The only peace from the drama seemed to be found in the grand garden at its centre, around which the Square was built.

"Which house is it?" Tommy asked as their little party trooped along the pavement.

Annie was pushing his wheelchair, Tommy having lost the use of his legs during the war, while Oliver Bankes came behind them dragging a trunk that had accompanied him all the way from Brighton. He had explained that it contained various pieces of photographic equipment including his camera. Clara marched ahead of the group looking out for door numbers, which seemed rather remiss in this neighbourhood.

"No. 50." She replied to Tommy's question over her shoulder, "But I can't see it."

Finally she had to nip into a high-end florist shop to make enquiries and was directed to a townhouse in the middle of the row. Clara knocked loudly on the door and waited for a response. The door was opened by a man in a suit who Clara took to be the butler. He stared down his nose at her.

"Yes?"

"Clara Fitzgerald and party. I am expected." Clara handed over her card.

The butler gave it a cursory look, then handed it back.

"Miss Sampford wants me to direct you to the drawing room. Would you come this way?"

Offering no assistance for either Tommy in his wheelchair (who had to negotiate several steps to reach the door) or Oliver and his trunk, the butler vanished into the house. Clara was not precisely astonished, more disappointed. She helped Annie with the chair and then returned to assist Oliver, who was complaining his glass plates would be all smashed at this rate. Once stationed in the hall she looked around for the butler, only to find him gone. Annie was giving a thoughtful look to the ornate staircase that dog-legged up to the next floor, wondering how on earth they would get Tommy up it.

"That gentleman is most inconsiderate." Clara snapped.

At that moment the butler emerged from an open doorway at the back of the hall.

"I have just enquired of Miss Sampford of the possibility of arranging for the young gentleman to have a room on the ground floor." He said, making no sign he had heard Clara, "She suggests the garden room would be most conveniently placed for such an arrangement. If you would follow me?"

Tommy gave Clara a laughing look. She ignored him, how was she to know the butler had gone off to adjust arrangements? Especially after he left them standing on the doorstep.

The garden room was set at the back of the house, off the main hall and down a second corridor. As its name implied it overlooked the back of the house, onto a neat garden. It was furnished in the fashions of the late Victorian period, with a great deal of lace edgings and knickknacks.

"I shall arrange for a bed to be brought down." The butler continued, "I shall also inform the maid to make up a fire. The water closet is just opposite, set behind the curve in the stairs. If the arrangements are suitable might I suggest you accompany me to the downstairs drawing room where I can fix you some drink?"

Oliver let go of the handle of his trunk with a loud thud.

"Sounds good to me."

"I'm sure it sounds good to all of us." Clara observed, "Please lead the way."

The butler ushered them to another room, this one overlooking the Square, which was equally decorated in the style of the previous century. A lively fire was burning in the hearth and gave the room a cosy air, while a large marmalade cat stretched out on a red-striped sofa and eyed them suspiciously.

"Miss Sampford will be with you shortly, might I serve you some drinks?"

The butler took their various requirements and opened a well-stocked drinks cabinet at the back of the room. Tommy, leaning precariously out of his wheelchair to catch a glimpse, reported to them all in a whisper that he could make out at least five types of whisky, several varieties of port and at least three types of sherry. Clara, who had merely asked for tonic water, wondered if the tee-totallers in the party were as well catered for as the alcoholics. Drinks served, the butler gave a stiff bow and excused himself from the room.

Oliver collapsed inelegantly into an armchair.

"That trunk was blooming heavy."

"I said to hire a porter at the station." Clara wandered to the fireplace and took a good look at the ornaments on display. She had a suspicion that each and every one was of a desirable and expensive nature.

"That butler gives me the creeps." Annie said.

"Everything gives you the creeps." Tommy responded teasingly, "He's pretty typical of your average Victorian butler. Probably been with the family centuries."

"Yes, but you haven't got to go down to the servants' quarters later and try and get along with him." Annie reminded him.

"Once you show the servants the cake you made you will have no problems." Tommy said with confidence.

Clara was studying some old photographs on a side table. She assumed they were of Miss Sampford's family, but only one showed a male sitter; a robust, middle-aged gentleman with a bald pate and grandiose side-whiskers. He looked out of the picture rather sternly, but Clara decided this meant very little as everyone stared out of Victorian photographs sternly, that was the problem with the long exposure times of the early cameras. Other pictures showed the same woman at different times of her life, presumably Miss Sampford. There was one of her as a girl, her hair long and her dress distinctly Victorian. Another showed her slightly older in a rowing boat with other girls, a third portrayed her in her forties astride a camel in some foreign country. A final picture showed her as an old woman, arm-in-arm with a much younger lady, grinning out at the photographer and proudly pointing out her 'Votes for Women' sash. Oh yes, thought Clara, I definitely like this woman.

The drawing room door opened and in stepped the lady in question. Clara turned sharply from the photos

13

and saw herself face-to-face with the subject of the images. She was a small woman, perhaps no more than five foot, but not wizened or hunched as some small old women become. She stood tall and proud, her hair swept up on top of her head in soft white folds. Her features were light, almost youthful, though her eyes were enlarged slightly by a small pair of round gold glasses. Miss Sampford stepped into the room with the soundless movement of a ballerina. There was no hint of her eighty years; her stride was as graceful as a young girl moving onto a dance floor. She took in her guests and smiled.

"Miss Fitzgerald."

"Miss Sampford."

They shook hands and Clara took the opportunity to introduce her party. Miss Sampford gave them all a nod.

"I wish you had said over the phone about Mr Fitzgerald's requirements. I would have had it all arranged." Miss Sampford said.

"It slipped my mind." Clara admitted, a tad embarrassed. Tommy gave a mock ashamed look.

"I see you all have drinks. I shall just pour myself one and join you. Please be seated, that goes for you too Annie." Miss Sampford moved off to the drinks cabinet and prepared herself a sizeable tumbler of whisky and water.

She had flummoxed Annie with her invitation to sit, the poor girl was glancing around trying to pick a spot to sit that was both out of the way, but not so far as to possibly offend Miss Sampford's hospitality. Clara gently motioned for her to sit next to Tommy, then positioned herself on the sofa next to the marmalade cat. The creature gave her a very unwelcoming hiss.

"Ignore Bartley." Miss Sampford returned with her drink and shooed the cat off the chair, "He is pedigree and exceedingly arrogant. He rarely bites, however."

Clara found that only partially comforting as the disagreeable cat stalked from the room.

"Now, I wish to say once again how pleased I am you could come. I appreciate it must have interrupted your Christmas plans."

"Once I read your letter I felt it was urgent I come down." Clara said, "Some of the things you wrote troubled me."

"I can assure you they also trouble me!" Miss Sampford sighed, "I really don't know what to make of this matter. I bought this house in 1909 and have never had any bother until now. I might have been able to persuade myself it was all nonsense had not my servants started leaving."

"And all have gone because of the ghost? You don't think they are using that as an excuse to leave?" Tommy interjected.

"I admit that is always a possibility. But I pay decent wages and this is a quiet little household. No, to lose so many and all for the same reason, it has to be more than just an excuse."

"What of long-standing servants? Have they said anything?" Clara asked.

"Mr Humphry, the butler who showed you in, dismisses the idea entirely. He is not the sort to believe in ghosts. It is Mrs James, my cook, who troubles me most. She worked under my mother and has been with me these last twenty or so years. She has never shown the slightest inclination towards trouble in all that time, but now to hear her talk of leaving for good because of a ghost... well, it astounds me."

"And the other servants?"

"I have two maids, Flora and Jane. They have been here just on a month and have made no mention of this ghost business to me, though, that does not mean they have not seen anything. I employ a gardener, but he only comes three times a week and lives out. The others have rooms on the attic floor. As far as I know the gardener has seen nothing, but then he is largely concerned with the outside of my home rather than the inside."

"You mentioned a nephew lives with you?"

"Yes, Elijah. He is supposed to be studying mathematics and stays with me when he has classes, but I'm not sure the boy is cut out for the rigours of number-work."

"How long has he been here on this visit?"

"Since October." Miss Sampford tilted her head towards Clara, "I see what you are suggesting, perhaps he is the cause? But the disturbances began in the summer when he was not here. I will introduce you to him at dinner and you can make of him what you will, after all, that is why I asked you here."

"Is there anyone else who regularly visits your household?"

"I do have a few friends who drop in from time-to-time. I'm afraid quite a number of others have passed away, when one gets to my age you spend a lot of time at funerals. I don't get out much these days. I suffer from a heart condition that makes it difficult. So making new acquaintances has proved problematic. I would say I get around one to two visits a week from friends, the most regular being Mrs Brown who usually pops in on a Sunday afternoon."

Clara made a note of this, not entirely sure it was relevant.

"Now, about the ghost?"

"Ah, I shall stop you there." Miss Sampford held up a finger to emphasize her point, "My nephew, upon learning of my invitation to you, has arranged that this ghost hunter of his shall come to dinner and, no doubt, he will also want to know about the ghost. I don't feel inclined to repeat the matter twice in one day, so I suggest you save your questions on that matter for tonight when we dine. I shall answer all then. For the moment I shall show you to your rooms, I have arranged that your maid will sleep in the dressing room off your bedroom Miss Fitzgerald."

Clara gave a smile to Annie, who was obviously relieved to learn she was not headed for the attic.

"Might I escort you there now? Humphry is working tirelessly on preparing the garden room for Mr Fitzgerald."

"Thank you for that." Tommy said.

"There is hardly a need for thanks, Mr Fitzgerald. A hostess must provide for her guests' needs. Let me show you upstairs Miss Fitzgerald, I have had your luggage taken to your rooms already."

Miss Sampford led the way up two flights of stairs, exiting onto the second floor and walking down a short corridor.

"Here is your room Miss Fitzgerald." She pushed open a door to reveal a neatly appointed bedroom, "Mr Bankes I have put you opposite."

"Thank you Miss Sampford, the room looks delightful." Clara stepped into her room and was pleased to smell it had been recently aired.

"I shall let you get on. Dinner is at seven, but I ask you to be down by six for drinks." Miss Sampford gave them another little nod and disappeared off down the corridor.

Clara admired her room, taking in its chintz wallpaper and four-poster bed. There were fresh flowers on the dresser and a smouldering fire in the hearth. Annie went past her and found the dressing room, set out with a single bed and a night-stand.

"We shall be very cosy, I reckon." She said.

"Indeed, I suspect, in fact, that I shall sleep too soundly for any ghost to disturb me."

"Don't jest about that Clara, you know I don't like ghosts."

"They aren't real Annie." Clara shrugged, "They are tricks of the light and such. No ghost is in this house, but there is someone playing tricks."

"For what end, Clara?"

Clara shook her head.

"At the best, simply for fun, but at the worst..." Clara sucked air through her teeth, "I just hope, for Miss Sampford's sake, that whoever is playing this game has nothing malicious on their mind."

"And if they do?"

Clara looked at the flowers on the dressing table and gave a long sigh.

"If they do, I just hope I can catch them before it is too late."

Chapter Three

Annie made her way down the back stairs to the kitchen, where she anticipated finding the household servants. She was nervous. Clara wanted her to win their trust and see what she could find out, along with persuading them not to flee the house should any more bizarre experiences befall them. Annie appreciated the trust and confidence Clara had placed in her, but she found the thought of striding into a strange kitchen a little daunting. In Annie's mind there was a whole world of difference between ordinary servants and those who worked in big houses in London. London servants were cosmopolitan, sophisticated, they knew all sorts of fancy French and Italian words for everyday foods like jelly and custard. Annie half imagined herself being assailed with all these foreign words without a clue as to what they meant. Perhaps they would ask her to bring a poussin from the pantry – she had read that word in a cook book – she was pretty certain it meant either a chicken or a fish. But what if she got it wrong in front of everyone? How mortifying!

Annie found herself in a long corridor, doors on either side of her, none were open and she didn't like to pry. Fortunately, as she strolled along, she came across the kitchen by chance. It was at the front of the house and extra windows had been let into the wall dividing it from the hall to provide light for the dim corridor. Annie peered through the windows and saw an older woman preparing pastry for a pie, while a maid scrubbed vigorously at a copper pot. Annie popped her head around the door and tapped lightly on the frame. The pastry cook glanced up.

"Who are you then?"

Annie stepped forward as confidently as she could manage.

"Annie Buckle, servant to Mr and Miss Fitzgerald."

"Ah, so you're with those guests the mistress asked down unexpectedly?" The cook thumped her ball of pastry down on a floured table, "I'm Mrs James, the cook. That over there is Flo."

Flo glanced up from her scrubbing and waved a wet hand.

"Very pleased to meet you. I brought something." In her hands Annie was carrying a white enamel cake tin – it was her poshest one, reserved for special cakes and items to be taken to the Church's yearly fete. She placed it on the table, "We came down on such short notice, seemed a shame to leave it at home after all the work gone into it."

She opened the tin and revealed her perfectly iced Christmas cake. White royal icing, as smooth as silk, covered the rich, whisky-soaked, fruit cake. A small marzipan robin nestled on a holly leaf right in the centre and Annie had spelt out 'season's greetings' in red icing around the bird. Mrs James looked down approvingly.

"That looks right nice. Done it yourself?"

"Absolutely." Annie affirmed.

"Got a clever hand there. I haven't iced our cake yet, maybe I'll leave it to you. Reckon you would do a finer job then I could with these big old things." Mrs James held up her floury hands and smiled.

Annie realised she had been accepted and beamed back.

"So your mistress is here to solve this ghost business?" Mrs James' became serious. She was a stout woman, as the best cooks tend to be, with a soft round face and a florid complexion. She had fading red hair, swept up under an old-fashioned mob-cap, and lively green eyes. When she smiled she revealed dimples and lines that indicated she was more inclined to be happy than sad and was clearly a woman content with her lot.

"Miss Fitzgerald doesn't believe in ghosts." Annie said honestly, "She thinks someone is playing tricks on your mistress."

"That crossed my mind at first." Mrs James suddenly could not meet Annie's eye, she grabbed up a rolling pin and went back to work.

"But now?" Annie asked.

Mrs James gave a strange look that seemed directed at Flo. The maid was focusing on her scrubbing, though she had already worked the copper to within an inch of its life.

"Flo, I don't have enough parsley for my pie. Go out to the green house and see if there is any left, would you?" Mrs James said.

Flo glanced at them both; she seemed aware she was wanted out of the way, but she made no comment and left the kitchen by the back door.

"She'll only be a moment." Mrs James spoke hastily, "Just between you and me, that mistress of yours better have her eyes open. There is something wrong in this house. I seen it for myself."

"What have you seen?"

"A shape, like a cloaked figure. In the second floor corridor. It was late afternoon and at this time of year the corridors are as pitch black as night. I had a candle because I had been to my room to fetch a book. I always read a little between lunch and dinner, if I have a chance. So I slipped to my room for a book and came down the back stairs and the door was open to the second floor corridor. I assumed either Flo or Jane had been careless about it and I went to shut it. That was when I saw someone standing in the dark corridor. Just standing. I knew it weren't Miss Sampford, it was too tall, so I imagined it was Mr Humphry on an errand. I closed the door and went downstairs. Imagine my surprise when I found Mr Humphry here at my very kitchen table going through the weekly accounts book! I tell you I started to feel quite queer. I told him what I had seen and he assumed there was a prowler in the house. But search as we might he never found anyone."

Mrs James rolled and rolled the pastry until it lay in a penny-thickness on the table. There was something determined and anxious in her thrusts of the pin. Annie suspected the woman was working hard to avoid showing that her hands were shaking.

"It could have been a prowler who spotted you and slipped out." Annie suggested.

"No, my dear, it was the ghost." Mrs James fell silent as the door opened again and Flo returned.

She walked to the table and deposited a handful of parsley.

"It's bitter out there, I think I should get the fires in the bedrooms lit." The maid said, her eyes turning to Annie, "Do you know what your mistress wants to wear tonight? We could hang it before the fire so it gets warm. This house holds the cold better than it does heat."

Annie sensed the girl was trying to get her away from the kitchen so they could talk. She wasn't about to miss the opportunity, especially as it seemed the servants were not talking about ghosts around each other if they could help it.

"Yes, that's a sound idea. I'll follow you up."

Flo grabbed some matches and a basket full of kindling, Annie gave a nod to Mrs James as she left. The cook resolutely focused on her pie, in a world of uncertainty pastry was at least one thing she could understand.

Flo didn't say anything until they were on the back stairs and heading upwards.

"Mrs James is very scared, we all are." She announced as they hit the first landing.

"No one has really explained why to me, yet." Annie answered.

"It's this ghost business. Your mistress might take it for nonsense, but believe me it's not. There are footsteps, things going missing, strange lights, groans in the night and now this figure!"

"Have you seen the ghost?"

"Not yet, and I don't want to. From what I hear the girl I replaced saw it one night and went stark raving mad."

Annie felt a shiver run up her spine.

"But it can't be real."

"Who says?"

Annie had no answer. They had reached the second floor and Flo was moving into the corridor.

"That is where Mrs James saw her." Flo pointed to a spot in the middle of the hallway.

"You think it's a woman?"

"I don't really know, but they say a woman was murdered in this house, so it has to be her ghost, right?" Flo walked down the corridor until she reached the spot where the ghost had supposedly stood, "I wouldn't be doing this if it were dark! But you don't see or hear anything during the day. See this room?" She indicated a doorway opposite her, "Miss Sampford keeps this as a library because no one dares sleep in it. That's where the murder happened."

Annie, a tad anxiously, peered into the room and saw walls lined with book cases and a desk in the middle facing the window. It was covered in papers and a black typewriter perched in the centre.

"Who was the woman?"

"No one seems really to know." Flo mused, "The scullery girl next door told me she were the lover of some lord who did away with her. But the man in the florist said he heard she were a servant girl who saw something she shouldn't."

"And her murderer?"

"No one can say, but I did hear tell that years ago a body was found buried at the bottom of the garden. Don't know what became of it though."

Annie stepped away from the room feeling sufficiently unnerved by stories of death and violence. She was starting to appreciate why Mrs James was so agitated.

"You see how the mistress has put your lady in the room nearly opposite the haunted one?" Flo asked, a glint of knowing in her eye, "She believes in this business more than she lets on."

"But, why now? The house has been quiet all these years, why has the ghost suddenly arisen?"

"My old mum says sometimes spirits get disturbed. Perhaps building work being done. Now just behind us there is a row of terraces and that Mr Hodge, a builder as what he calls himself, has been knocking things down and building things up. He is working right near our garden where the bones of that murdered girl were said to have been found. I think he has disturbed something."

That was enough for Annie; the thought of the dead rising from their graves because they had been disturbed chilled her to the bone. She headed for Clara's bedroom and Flo followed. For a moment Annie was too bemused and scared to speak. Flo began placing the kindling in the hearth and the distraction of such a mundane task began to calm Annie.

"Does it come every night?" She asked, thinking she would need more rational information to satisfy Clara, talk of half-remembered murder stories and nameless suspects would not impress.

"Most nights." Flo said, stacking a piece of kindling, "Miss Sampford goes to bed around nine, and usually I'm done with my chores by eleven. Me and Jane go up to bed together, Mrs James comes next, then Mr Humphry after he has locked the house up tight. It usually begins about an hour after we are all abed." Flo paused in her work, trying her hardest to remember everything perfectly, "About one o'clock the footsteps begin. Thud, thud, thud.

Heavy they are, like someone in boots. Jane thinks it is the sound of the murderer revisiting the scene of the crime. Then there will be other noises; bangs, crashes, doors opening and closing, but nothing is ever amiss when you look the next morning. Sometimes there is a voice muttering, once we heard a scream. On another occasion all the bells in the house began to ring at once."

"Where does this happen?"

Flo gave an apologetic smile.

"Second floor, always the second floor. Miss Sampford has the room at the end. If it ever moved up them stairs I wouldn't be here, I tell you."

Annie sat on the bed and gave a little groan. Not only was she sleeping on the floor the ghost inhabited but opposite the very room it haunted. She wondered if Clara would mind if she insisted on having a room in the attic?

"Have I worried you?" Flo stood, looking sad.

"No, don't worry about it. Clara will probably attack your ghost with a poker if it comes too near."

Flo cocked her head, intrigued at the sudden lapse in formality, but she said nothing.

"Mr Sampford is bringing in a ghost hunter. I hear they are going to do a séance with a real medium."

"Oh Clara will hate that!" Annie almost snorted at the thought, "You know she once had a case where she had to solve the murder of a medium."

"Really? Is your mistress right clever then?"

"Very!"

"And does she know how to deal with ghosts?"

Annie couldn't answer that. Clara was many things, but her interest in the paranormal was limited.

"As I said, there are very few things that don't get scared when Clara is wielding a poker."

"Even a ghost?"

"I guess. Ghosts are just people too, or rather, once were."

Flo looked as unconvinced as Annie sounded.

Chapter Four

Clara wore her blue dress to dinner. It was not as figure-hugging as some and had a flattering pleat in the side. Clara was well aware that despite her best efforts she would never be one of those girls who had perfected the 'waif-look' and could wear the straightest of dresses without showing off even a hint of curves. She met Oliver on the staircase; he was looking very striking in an evening suit and bowtie.

"Very smart Mr Bankes."

"I could say the same Miss Fitzgerald." He offered her his arm, "Have you met Mr Elijah Sampford yet?"

"No, have you?"

"I spotted him in the library about an hour ago. He was talking to a strange-looking man with white whiskers."

"Ah." Clara thought about this, "Either one of the other Sampford relatives or the ghost hunter he talked of employing."

They reached the bottom of the staircase and found Tommy waiting for them. Mr Humphry was in charge of the handles of his wheelchair.

"What ho!" Called Tommy, "Are your rooms as snug as mine?"

"I am opposite the haunted library." Clara announced with pleasure, "Annie is quite beside herself."

"Poor thing, send her to me if she can't stand it." Tommy gave a wink.

"If we might all venture into the drawing room?" Mr Humphry spoke with his same rather superior tone and not a whiff of emotion on his face, "Miss Sampford appreciates punctuality."

"Roll on Jeeves!" Tommy said teasingly.

This raised a strange look on the butler's face, somewhere between bemusement and a sneer of disapproval. He coughed awkwardly and then pushed Tommy towards the drawing room. Clara and Oliver followed behind.

Miss Sampford was sitting by the fireplace trying to look as interested as she could while a man in a tweed suit was going into great detail about experiments he had done with magnets and their influence on the environment. There were lots of words such as 'ether', 'clairvoyance', 'mesmeric powers' and 'electro-magnetism' being bandied about.

"Ah, Miss Fitzgerald!" Miss Sampford sprang to her feet, interrupting the man in tweed mid-sentence, as she spotted Clara, "May I introduce Mr Andrews? He is a ghost hunter…"

"Psychical investigator." Mr Andrews interjected promptly. He was the man with the white-whiskers Oliver had spotted upstairs.

"Ahem, yes, a psychical investigator. This, Mr Andrews, is Miss Clara Fitzgerald, a private investigator who has come to assist with this matter."

Mr Andrews stood. He was a little shorter than Clara and quite pot-bellied. He had lost most of the hair on his head, but had a fine full moustache and, of course, those side whiskers – all snow white in colour. He smiled, but there was something in the expression that made it appear far from genial. Despite his rather round and soft appearance he struck Clara as being a very hard man.

Clara held out her hand to shake. Mr Andrews' face darkened for an instant and he ignored the gesture pointedly.

"An investigator? And what does your husband make of that?" He asked.

"I believe I said she was Miss Fitzgerald." Miss Sampford admonished him.

"Oh I see, one of those ladies who find it necessary to dabble in scientific matters until a man comes along to occupy their time. I suppose you think you should have the right to vote too?"

"Well the government has seen fit to give it to every other idiot going. I am presuming you vote Mr Andrews."

"Quite." Mr Andrews gave a cough, "And what precise expertise are you bringing to this case?"

"I'm sorry, but is there such a thing as expertise in ghost-hunting?"

Mr Andrews laughed.

"Naturally, dear girl. Not that I would expect you to understand."

"I just didn't imagine you could have an expert in things that didn't exist. Surely in that case we could have experts on unicorns and mermaids?"

"I think you are mocking me Miss Fitzgerald and in the process showing your ignorance."

"On the contrary Mr Andrews." Clara smiled, "I take all my investigations very seriously. Are you associated with the SPR?"

Mr Andrews bristled.

"No. I find that organisation rather stuffy."

"What a shame. I was hoping you would introduce me to Sir Arthur Conan Doyle, he has done so much for the Spiritualist movement."

"The man is a bombastic cretin." Mr Andrews spluttered.

"Yes, but look how well he has done! Who has not heard of Sherlock Holmes, perhaps you should ask him for a tip or two?"

Mr Andrews was almost purple with outrage.

"You do look quite queer Mr Andrews." Clara said knitting her eyebrows into a look of concern, "Are you sensing a presence?"

"Yes, a very disagreeable one." Andrews snorted.

"How odd, I have been sensing one just the same since I entered this room. I do hope he goes soon." Clara gave a bright smile and excused herself to fetch a drink.

Miss Sampford joined her by the drinks cabinet.

"Reminds me of the days before the war." She said with a grin, "Taking all those chauvinistic fools in government down a peg or two."

"I saw the picture of your glory days." Clara answered, accepting the glass of tonic water Miss Sampford offered.

"Those were the days! I threw a brick through the house window of a High Court Judge." She glowed with pride, "I was sent to prison for it."

"There is still so much to achieve though before we can consider ourselves equals in every aspect of life to men."

"Yes, and it is all beyond me now." Miss Sampford suddenly looked sad, "To think of all I went through and here I am now scared by a silly trick of my imagination."

Clara placed a hand on her arm comfortingly.

"Who said it was your imagination? I'll solve this Miss Sampford."

"Thank you Clara, may I call you Clara? I have more faith in you than that fool with his electro-magnetism and invisible agents." Miss Sampford gave a brave laugh, "Now, let me introduce my nephew."

Elijah Sampford was at that age when the body seemed to stretch upwards producing a lanky-looking youth, with not enough apparent muscle to account for his ability to stand upright. He was all elbows and knees, a little ungainly, but with a hint of the man he would soon grow into. He had a very small, oval head on a tall neck, his close cropped and slicked back hair making it look like a pea perched on the tip of a knife. He wore small round glasses very similar to his aunt's and was very exuberant in greeting Clara.

"I'm so glad you could come! Auntie said you are the finest, I say this is going to be such a good show!" He shook Clara's hand enthusiastically, "Have you met Mr Andrews? I know him through the university. He is a friend of Professor Graves who teaches biology and sometimes he comes in and borrows things from the labs. He jumped at the chance to investigate our ghost."

"I can imagine. " Clara smiled, "And what do you make of the haunting?"

"Well, I try to remain sceptical." Elijah nodded seriously, "But really it is very hard with all the strange happenings going on. I rather like the idea of a tormented spirit, it's rather interesting. I've read all the books by Mr Frederick Myers and Mr William Stead on the subject. What a shame Stead died on the Titanic! He would have loved this!"

Clara found it hard to stem the tide of Elijah's enthusiasm.

"And you have seen the ghost?"

"Good lord, no! Damn shame too. But I've heard strange noises, sounds like footsteps mainly. And I once found the room to my door open when I could have sworn I closed it."

"That could quite simply be a case of the servants going in and being careless." Miss Sampford suggested.

"Really Auntie, you must always dismiss my experiences."

"I apologise Elijah. I only say it to try and comfort myself. I hope there is nothing at all in this matter except imagination."

"Don't worry, old girl, we have the best minds here to deal with the case."

"Yes." Miss Sampford spoke so only Clara could hear, "And then there is Mr Andrews."

A gong rang out somewhere in the house and Mr Humphry appeared at the door.

"May I ask you all to make your way to the dining room?" He asked the assorted guests.

Everyone filtered through to a high-ceilinged dining room with a precisely laid table. Clara imagined Humphry had been going about with his ruler to ensure every fork and spoon was exactly in its place before summoning them in. Mr Andrews was first to his place. He immediately removed the neatly folded napkin from his plate and wedged it into his shirt collar. Then his knife and fork were swopped from their correct sides and the smaller pieces of cutlery piled up onto a side plate.

"Can't be dealing with all these silly forks." He declared to the room.

Mr Humphry was hardly able to hide his chagrin at the sight of his precision table setting so disrespected. Miss Sampford took her place at the head of the table, so Andrews was on her left and Clara on her right. Tommy was wheeled next to Andrews and Oliver was seated by Clara, while Elijah sat at the bottom of the table facing his aunt. Humphry could be heard giving a faint sigh as he walked round with the wine.

Clara took her napkin and draped it in her lap.

"Is it now time to hear about the ghost?" She asked Miss Sampford.

"Let poor Humphry serve the pea soup first." Their hostess replied, "Mr Andrews are you aware that is a dessert spoon not a soup spoon in your hand?"

Andrews hastily dropped the offending piece of silver and picked up another. Miss Sampford gave him a small nod. Humphry served the soup which was a vivid green with a swirl of cream in the centre. It had a faint hint of mint. Clara took a bread roll from a plate the butler offered her. For a few moments there was silence as everyone settled to their food. They quickly discovered that Mr Andrews had an annoying tendency to slurp.

"I suppose I should start my story, as we are all suitably gathered." Miss Sampford began, giving a hard look at Andrews' slurping, "I have to ask you will not consider me foolish as I speak, I shall give you the facts and not my interpretation and then you will hopefully understand why I have become so unnerved."

"It is natural to be worried under the circumstances." Mr Andrews said, making an effort to be genuinely considerate, "Especially at your age."

Miss Sampford masterfully ignored him.

"The matter began back in June. I actually made a note of the date subsequently and I consulted my diary before coming down tonight. It was the 21 June and it happened to be the summer equinox. Whether that is significant is for you to decide. In any case I was lying in bed around two in the morning and I heard the noise of a door opening and closing on the floor below me. I found that rather odd as everyone was abed, or at least I thought they were. Naturally I imagined we had a burglar and I lay very still to try and hear for someone moving about, but there was not another sound. Neither did I hear anyone climb the stairs as if heading for the servants' attic. I must have lain awake for an hour expecting to hear more, but there was nothing and finally I convinced myself I had been mistaken."

"When you went downstairs the next day was anything out of place?" Clara asked, delicately dabbing up the last of her soup with a corner of bread.

"No. All the doors were shut and locked, nothing was moved or missing. Naturally I assumed I was mistaken. But that night I heard the noise again, a door opening and closing. I listened hard and thought I also heard muffled footsteps, but they were very faint. The following morning I asked Humphry if any of the servants had got up in the night, but he assured me they had not. When the next night came I was determined to be wide awake to hear the noise, perhaps, I told myself it was an echo from outside that I was misinterpreting. You see, at this time, I had no thoughts of ghosts, but I was just curious.

"The night came and I sat up in a chair with a candle, reading a book. I watched the clock carefully and as two o'clock approached I put down my book and listened as intently as I could. This time I heard footfalls first, then a door opened and closed, as before. I could not say which door, but it seemed right beneath me, which would make it the upstairs drawing room. After that I heard what sounded like shuffling and then footsteps again, then nothing. It was all very curious and I resolved to go down at once and discover who was about. I wondered if one of my servants was suffering from an extended bout of indigestion and was walking about to ease it. I headed downstairs as quietly as I could, so I would not disturb the walker, for I still had to wonder if we had an intruder abroad. I reached the first floor and saw not a soul. Every door was closed and locked and the hallway empty."

"Did you use the main stairs or the back stairs?" Clara had started to make notes in a book she kept for such a purpose.

"The main stairs, naturally."

"So, theoretically, if a person had gone up the back stairs while you were coming down the main stairs, you would have missed each other?"

Miss Sampford had to admit that was possible.

"I see you are not very familiar with the typical conditions of a haunting, Miss Fitzgerald." Andrews sat back in his chair, hands folded over his stomach, a smug look on his face, "If you were, you would be aware that what Miss Sampford has described is the most common way a haunting begins."

"Do you deny a living person might have made the sounds?" Clara countered.

"Facts are facts, Miss Fitzgerald, clearly the matter did not remain as footsteps alone, and what I am saying is that in all the cases I have investigated the majority of genuine hauntings have begun with mundane noises such as footsteps and doors opening."

"So because, in your experience, hauntings begin with footsteps you are excluding the possibility that a human agent was innocently behind the matter?"

"If it was a human in this household why did they not come forward and say so?"

"Unfortunately I can think of several reasons." Clara said, "None of which involve the paranormal, but do imply subterfuge. Of course we might also have a sleepwalker in our midst."

"I used to sleepwalk." Elijah piped up from the bottom of the table, flashing a sheepish grin at everyone, "But I wasn't here in June. Sorry, that was a very pointless interruption."

"Perhaps we should let Miss Sampford continue?" Clara suggested.

"Perhaps indeed." Andrews agreed, still with that smug look on his face.

Miss Sampford started once more on her task.

"This mystery of the opening and closing doors, followed by footsteps, went on for another week, until I was quite bored with the matter. I investigated a few more times and found nothing and eventually gave up, resolving it was a queer fluke of sound, perhaps coming from next door. As, up until then, everything had occurred on the first floor I was not really perturbed and I began to ignore it, and then things began to occur on the second floor, where I sleep. I had a young maid at the time, she had been with the household about a month and though a little on the silly side I had no reason to complain about her. Then abruptly she handed in her notice one morning, naturally I asked what could be the matter, all had seemed well up until that point. 'I can't abide that thing anymore.' She told me, I asked her to clarify what thing she meant. It took a bit of persuasion to get it out of her, but at last she explained; 'Whenever I goes on the second floor I feel I am being watched. It's worst in the library, when I bend to set the hearth to rights I would swear on my mother's grave someone is leaning over me and I hear breathing.' Had I not heard the strange noises in the night myself, I might have thought her mad. In any case I found it quite impossible to make her stay."

Miss Sampford paused as Humphry entered with a large Beef Wellington, followed by the maid Jane carrying a large tureen of mashed potatoes in one hand and a dish of mixed vegetables in the other. For several moments the guests had to wait impatiently for the continuation of the story. Mr Humphry seemed inclined to serve very slowly, but at last the food was on the plates and the servants temporarily removed themselves. Miss Sampford passed a gravy boat to Clara and gave her a smile. Then she picked up her fork and started forth with her tale again.

"Maids are a nuisance to hire in this day and age, but I soon had another girl installed in the house. I had quietly apprised Humphry and Mrs James on the strange matter of the last girl feeling watched and it was understood the new maid should not be told anything. In the meantime, I made a point of being on the second floor during the hour the maid cleaned and set the fires in the rooms there. I looked upon it this way, should this new maid feel watched she would put it down to my presence rather than something supernatural. I spent my mornings in the library and, in actual fact, it proved quite advantageous as it gave me the opportunity to work on a book of memoirs I had been intending to complete for years."

Miss Sampford smiled at her guests as she sliced into a gently poached carrot.

"Remind me to show you my work later Clara, I hope to have it published before I die, all the other ex-suffrage girls are doing it."

"I imagine there are quite some stories to tell." Clara nodded.

"It is the reason I get so bothered about being troubled by a ghost. After all I went through, why should I be afraid of something I can't even see?"

"I think you will find that is exactly the reason people are afraid of ghosts." Andrews reinserted himself into the conversation, "Ghosts combine our greatest fears; the unknown and the unspeakable."

"Not to mention they only show up at night!" Elijah piped up, "I'm dreadfully afraid of the dark as it is."

"That is actually a common error perpetrated by novelists." Andrews spoke with a know-it-all swagger to his voice, "Ghosts are equally likely to appear during the day."

"Which I believe I demonstrated when I explained about the maid?" Miss Sampford said, "She certainly wasn't cleaning at night when she felt a 'presence', as the Spiritualists call it. Unfortunately, my hopes that these strange problems would leave with the maid were misguided. The doors shutting and footsteps pacing continued, but now they were becoming clearer and more determined. I sleep alone on the second floor and it was most disturbing to lie in my bed and realise that someone was coming up the stairs from the floor below. Each night the footsteps seemed to get closer to my own room and each night I would bounce out of my bed, grab a candle and dash out into the hall and see nothing. I was finding it very hard to convince myself this was still all imagination.

"Then the new maid came to me with her notice. Her explanation was that someone had attempted to push her down the back stairs more than once. She had distinctly felt a shove to her back; thankfully it did not cause her to fall. But she turned around to confront the culprit and found no one there. She was made of stern stuff, but after three attempts like this she could no longer stand it. Now I was truly flummoxed, I knew no one else in the household would play such dangerous games, so what could I blame it on?

"Once again I hired a new maid on the strict instructions she was not to know about the strange occurrences. This girl lasted almost a month before she informed me she could stand the house no longer, she described the pushing on the stairs, the feeling of a presence and then added that one day she had seen a pair of red eyes glowering at her from the open cellar door. This is the pattern that has repeated itself up to today. I finally decided to hire two maids at once, so they could accompany each other around the house. I can see you thinking how desperate that is, but I can't keep having maids leave."

"And have Jane or Flo reported anything?" Clara asked.

"Not so far. They know about it, of course, after the third maid I knew it would be far-fetched to try and keep the matter completely secret. People talk, after all."

"What about the night-time disturbances?" Andrews queried as he helped himself to more gravy on his potatoes.

Miss Sampford hesitated, she clearly was not sure how to proceed, perhaps even afraid she would be laughed at by some of her guests. Her eyes met Clara's.

"You can only state what you have seen or heard." Clara said gently, "Then it is for us to interpret it according to our own prejudices."

"For once, I agree with you." Andrews gave Clara an insincere smile. She ignored him.

"I must insist that you believe me when I say these next things occurred when I was awake." Miss Sampford was almost pleading with her guests to understand her, "The footsteps had been coming closer and closer to my room, but I never saw anyone, try as I might to jump out just as the footsteps were nearest. This grew rather tiresome after a while, and I resolved once more to ignore the sounds, whatever they were. It was the second night after I had made that resolution that I discovered what the owner of the footsteps intended all along, had I not kept interrupting them by springing out into the hallway. I lay in my bed, and I swear Miss Fitzgerald that I heard the footsteps stop right outside my door and the handle turned."

Someone gasped. Apparently it was the easily over-wrought Elijah.

"Can you imagine what I felt at that moment? I leapt out of my bed and I twisted the key in the lock and heard the clunk as the levers fell into place. The handle had stopped turning and for a moment I thought my heart would stop beating, silly old fool that I am! I checked all my windows and then sat up all night in my bed waiting for the creeper to return. So far the ghost, if that is what it is, has only attempted to open my door once more. Fortunately I had locked it. The odd thing was, I heard footsteps approaching my room, but I never heard them leave."

"What you describe is the classic pattern of a restless spirit haunting." Andrews leaned forward, almost letting his lapels fall on his empty plate, "In fact, it strikes me as what we call in this business, a poltergeist!"

"I've read about those." Tommy had been carefully keeping silent through dinner mainly because, owing to his cold, it was rather difficult to eat and breathe at the same time, "Harry Price has described the poltergeist as an entity springing out of nothing."

"Pah! Harry Price." Andrews snorted, "He is nothing more than a trumped up paper bag salesman. No, I have spent considerable time observing such hauntings and I can state, categorically, that behind them is a thinking spirit."

"So you don't think it a result of disturbances in the atmosphere?"

"Humph, naturally not." Andrews waved a hand dismissively.

Tommy was prevented from replying by the arrival of pudding; a rather over-decorated blancmange in the shape of a turreted castle. The guests were given a moment to marvel at the delight, which wobbled pinkly, before it was served into manageable portions. Once everyone was silenced Miss Sampford continued her dialogue.

"Beyond the turning door handle I have had one other experience which truly unnerved me. It was late one night and I had been suffering with a slight fever which made me restless. I awoke around two o'clock and to my alarm there was a veiled figure standing over my bed and staring down at me. I rang the bell next to my bed at once and then, much to my subsequent embarrassment, I hid my head beneath the blankets. When Humphry arrived there was nobody there, but I was so certain..." Miss Sampford hesitated for just a moment, "I am not the only one to have seen the ghost. Mrs James is quite convinced she has seen someone walking about the second floor when no one should be there. She has described them as tall and possibly wearing a hat and large coat, or a cape, as they appear rather shapeless. Over the last month she has witnessed this at least five times and on each occasion the figure was outside my bedroom door. Mrs James is a brave woman, but nothing would compel her to confront the figure, so on each instance she has rushed to summon help, usually in the form of Humphry. On every occasion he has searched the house thoroughly and found no one.

"Then there is the experience of my dear friend Mrs Chambers, who came to call on me Wednesday last. She is inordinately fond of ginger biscuits, and when the maids served tea I was quite aggrieved to see they had placed bourbon creams in the biscuit jar, rather than the ginger ones I had requested. I rose to personally attend to the matter and left Mrs Chambers alone for around five minutes. When I returned she seemed a little ruffled, but she said nothing. Then, as I was offering her a biscuit she asked if I had another visitor that day. I answered no, only her. 'Then it must have been a maid I saw at the door,' She said, hesitantly, 'only, it was very odd as they seemed to have a traveling cloak on, remember the old ones our grandmamas would wear to go out in the cold or rain. It covered them from head to foot.' Where did you see this person? I asked, naturally thinking of the strange happenings. But, I told myself, it might have been someone coming to call then seeing I already had a guest, leaving. 'Oh, they opened the door.' Mrs Chambers said, 'Just a fraction as if they wanted to see who was here. I didn't see them direct, you understand, but spotted them in the mirror over the fireplace.' She pointed at the old big mirror I have hung there, 'They were gone within moments.' I decided to brush off the incident, concurring with my friend that it must have been another visitor who had popped in briefly. But I suspect neither of us was completely convinced. As you may have noted, this mysterious figure bore a very similar appearance to that which Mrs James had described concerning the person on the second floor."

Miss Sampford finished her story and turned her attention to her blancmange. No one seemed inclined to speak. Clara was mulling over all the possibilities the story suggested, the one she was carefully excluding was that what Mrs Chambers had seen was a ghost. Nothing she had heard, so far, required a paranormal explanation to account for it. Finally Andrews broke the silence.

"You have presented a most vivid account Miss Sampford, truly engaging." He said with condescending praise, "What you have described, as you may imagine, does not surprise me. Like a doctor who has seen many diseases and is very familiar with the symptoms of the commoner sorts of illness, I am experienced enough to recognise the signs of a standard haunting. I propose that you have a restless soul in your home who, with a bit of guidance, may be persuaded to leave. But first, to confirm my diagnosis, I shall set up some equipment on the second floor, then I shall summon my assistants tomorrow to prepare for an all-night vigil. Lastly I shall use the services of a medium to perform the necessary exorcism." As he spoke, the clock in the hall chimed nine o'clock. Andrews gave a little start, "Good heavens! I must get prepared, my equipment takes considerable time to set-up and I cannot afford to miss a moment. Thank you for the dinner Miss Sampford, please excuse me."

Andrews cast down his napkin and started from the table.

"Might I be of any help?" Oliver offered, rising too, "I am a photographer, so I am good with technical equipment."

Andrews looked at him suspiciously, no doubt seeing him as the enemy, associated as he was with Clara. At the same time, quite a few of his pieces of equipment were heavy and difficult to manoeuvre alone. Reluctantly Andrews accepted the offer of help. The two men left.

"By Jove, how exciting!" Elijah said, his round face beaming with enthusiasm, "How on earth will I sleep tonight knowing there is a trap set for the ghost?"

"I am sure you will manage it." His aunt said gently, "Why don't you take Mr Fitzgerald for a drink and a cigar? I wish to speak with Clara privately."

"Quite! Quite! I forget my manners when I get excited." Elijah jumped from the table and grabbed the handles of Tommy's wheelchair, "I fancy a whisky, perhaps that will help me sleep. Do ghosts still come if you remain awake for them? Oh gosh, what a silly question!"

With this barrage of talk (and a wistful look at Clara) Tommy was swept away. Miss Sampford rose and Clara followed.

"Let's go to the snug." Miss Sampford said, "I always feel safe there."

Chapter Five

"This used to be a study, but I had it converted to a private sitting room and call it my 'snug'." Miss Sampford showed Clara into a panelled room with a glowing fire and large, comfortable-looking, leather armchairs. The room smelt warm and faintly of lavender. More photographs of Miss Sampford and her family hung on the walls, giving a homely feel. Miss Sampford directed Clara to one armchair and then took the other for herself. Giving a small sigh she sank into it.

"Entertaining grows rather tiresome when you are old." She smiled at her guest, "I am so dull these days, but there is nothing that gives me more pleasure than a quiet dinner followed by reading in my snug until I fall asleep."

"That sounds most pleasurable." Clara replied, "I suspect most people entertain for appearance's sake rather than out of sheer enjoyment. So many of them seem decidedly stressed when you appear for dinner, as if they would much rather not have guests at all."

Miss Sampford laughed.

"The world is a strange place! We spend so much time doing things we don't really want to because we feel we should. Only once one gets so old that nobody cares about you anymore, can you at last do as you please. But, of course, by then you are too old."

"I feel you underestimate the number of people who care about you, Miss Sampford."

Miss Sampford gave a derisive huff.

"Most of the people who truly cared are dead, I am sad to say. See all those photographs on the wall?" Miss Sampford pointed to the framed pictures, "So many dear friends and loved ones no longer living, I look up and see a wall of the dearly departed."

"Then, may I suggest you have some new photographs taken of the living people who are with you today. Elijah for instance?"

"You make it very hard for an old woman to feel sorry for herself." The old lady said without anger.

"My father always used to say if we are unhappy with our lives then it is up to us to change them. And if we are not prepared to do that, then self-pity is really a waste of time." Clara sighed, "Not that I don't indulge in self-pity from time to time. It can be strangely enjoyable."

"You would have made a good suffragette Clara." Miss Sampford grinned, "Those were grand days for women who think like you and I. Days when you felt you had a purpose."

"And now women have the vote, or at least some do."

"And my purpose has gone. Oh, but you will now tell me I must find a new purpose!"

"Absolutely!" Clara chuckled, "How dull if we only ever have one purpose in life? In any case, I thought you were writing your memoirs?"

"Oh yes, but do you suppose anyone will want to read them?"

"I cannot say for certain, but I think it very foolish to allow such important memories to slip away and be forgotten."

"Then when my book is done you shall have the first copy, signed, naturally."

"I shall look forward to it."

Miss Sampford stood up and rang the bell for the servants. Jane appeared momentarily and Miss Sampford ordered a pot of tea, before she returned to her seat.

"Elijah prefers coffee after dinner, but I find it makes me wakeful." She complained lightly.

"Tea is much preferable." Clara assured her, "Now, while we are away from that awful Mr Andrews, why don't we discuss your other concerns? The ones of a corporeal nature?"

"That Mr Andrews is ghastly, of course he might be good at his job." Miss Sampford settled herself in her chair, "But my other concerns, yes, those I must explain. What an awful business."

"You mentioned in your letter that you wondered if someone was trying to make it impossible for you to live here?"

"Yes, a gentleman by the name of Edward Mollinson. He is a builder, or so I understand, and has bought several properties both in the square and in the streets around for, I believe they call it, redevelopment. He actually owns number 49, next door. I hear he plans to turn it into a hotel, but the property is not large enough for his schemes, so he has been badgering me for months to buy number 50. If he has his way he will merge 49 and 50 into one enormous monstrosity, though I dare say the shopkeepers will be happy."

"And you refuse to sell." Clara stated.

"I didn't buy this house to move out in my last years. I am content here, I have it arranged as I want. I don't have any desire to go house-hunting at my time of life."

"How has Mr Mollinson reacted to this?"

"Mostly he just voices his annoyance. He is one of those smarmy businessmen who think they can persuade anyone to do anything if they just offer enough charm and money. I can't say he has been aggressive in any manner, though I doubt he likes me much."

"And when did he last visit?"

Miss Sampford considered the question, scrolling through the last few weeks in her mind. While she did so the tea arrived. Clara offered to pour out two cups while Miss Sampford thought about her answer.

"I believe his last call was either late September or early October." The old woman said at last, "It was his standard visit asking if I had changed my mind or if there was anything he could do to encourage me to sell."

"Had he paid any other calls during the time of the haunting, or perhaps just before?"

"I think he called in July, he roughly comes every two months. His visits coincide with his inspection of the work being carried out next door. As you may imagine, with my hesitation to sell, this has been slow. Now you mention it, I do believe he paid a call just before the noises began. It was one of the rare occasions he let his temper fray. His men had been gutting number 49 and he wanted to move on with the project. He was quite surly when he demanded to know why I could not be more reasonable. I asked him why his desires were so much more important than my own."

"That is interesting. What about on his later visits? Did he ever discuss the ghost?"

"Actually…" Miss Sampford's face lit up as if she had just recalled something, "You have reminded me why I began to suspect him in the first place. The October visit, his last one, he was in a rather cocky mood, much more jolly than normal and, when we were sat drinking tea, he once again began rambling on about his projects, he suddenly asked how the ghost of Berkeley Square suited me. I was a little stunned and I asked him whatever could he mean? He replied that he had heard I had a ghost who rattled doorknobs and stomped about. He knew I had lost several maids and wondered aloud how I was managing as an older lady in a house with such confusion. He then suggested a move to a modern property would be much more soothing. I stoutly denied everything, but it did make me wonder. I had quite forgotten that conversation until now. I must admit I have had quite a number of visitors wanting to know of the ghost. So many I started to lose track of who I had and hadn't spoken to on the subject."

"May I ask, if the man's offers are so disagreeable, why you keep entertaining him?" Clara asked carefully.

"Unfortunately the answer to that is not greatly to my credit." Miss Sampford actually looked abashed, "I rather enjoy taunting him. He reminds me so much of those sweet-tongued politicians of the 'teens, who assured us again and again votes for women were being discussed and then quietly let it drop. I suppose it was very unkind, but a little touch of mischief entered my soul and I couldn't resist."

"No matter, Miss Sampford. He had it coming for pestering you. But what about your other suspicions?"

"Ah." Miss Sampford stared into her tea for a moment, then she stood and went to the wall of photographs. She plucked down one and handed it to Clara. It showed a stout Victorian gentleman, the sort with big whiskers and a permanent place in the local hunt. He held a pipe in one hand and stared intimidatingly at the camera, "That is my father Colonel Sampford, fourth baron of Wimfrey. To explain my other concerns I need to first elaborate on my relationship with my parents.

"I was an only daughter out of five sons, all my brothers lived into adulthood. The eldest, Henry, took over the estate and became the fifth baron. Upon his death, his son William Henry acquired the title and moved into the house with his wife Amelia. You shall meet them tomorrow when they arrive for Christmas."

"They are your nephew and niece-in-law." Clara placed the photograph on a side table.

"Yes. My other brothers went into various occupations suitable for the sons of a baron; the army, the Church, the law. That left me. Father had left me in no doubt that he expected I should marry when the time was right, probably to one of our cousins. He was very despondent when no marriage proposals came my way, naturally I never informed him of the ones I turned down." Miss Sampford winked mischievously, "Father's attitude was that all his children should be independent of him and the estate, except Henry. As a woman I did not have the option of earning my living in a way deemed respectable to my father, my only choice was therefore marriage. But as the years ticked by with no proposal, so father became more and more concerned. Finally he summoned me one day and asked if I ever intended to find a husband. When I replied I did not there was a dreadful row and father kicked me out of the house, just like that! Thankfully, my brother John lived nearby and I went to him. He approached father on my behalf. Henry was also there, and there was a heated discussion over my future. Father and Henry felt I was being deliberately obstinate, John defended me and demanded to know what father planned should he die while I was still unmarried. He couldn't leave me with nothing, he insisted, I was his flesh and blood after all.

"I can only imagine the challenge of that discussion. Father could be pig-headed and Henry was little better. The estate was eating money faster than it came in from various family investments and father's biggest concern was that I would be a drain on the estate resources once he was gone and possibly force Henry to sell the estate, which had been in the family for three centuries."

"That is an awful way to think." Clara said, deeply saddened by the story.

"Can you see why I was so adamant women should be equal to men? So often our feelings and desires are ignored because of financial considerations, which would not be necessary if we had the same powers to earn a living as men do. Of course, father's behaviour upset me deeply and our relationship was never quite the same again. John, however, was extremely persuasive. Before the end of the day he had not only persuaded father to let me back home, should I wish, but he had him agree to a provision in his will that would allow me a yearly income until my death, if I did not marry. Should I marry the provision was lost. Henry was furious as he felt it gave me every incentive not to find a husband, but as I was already 39 and so far unmarried, John argued that it was unlikely I would now find a husband. Does that not sound awful? Even my favourite brother could not fathom myself being attractive to a man once my youth was gone."

Miss Sampford gave a long sigh.

"I don't have a picture of John. He died in 1885 and the only photos were in my brother Henry's possession. My father died in 1881 and since then I have been living on my annual allowance. He had also left a small pension for my mother. When she died in 1908 she left what money she had to me and it was enough, with the savings I had carefully accrued, to buy this property. Henry found it most irritating that I continued to live on in fine health, draining his resources. He had to sell off a portion of the estate lands for a housing development. Needless to say that put me even further out of favour. When he died in 1915 he was still bemoaning the fact I was alive and unmarried. Apparently, so I am told, he mumbled about it on his death bed."

"I can't imagine how that must have felt." Clara shook her head, "I suspect you are going to tell me that William Henry shares his late father's views?"

"Indeed, and with the awful burden of death duties after his father's death, he has found himself having to tighten his belt considerably. My continual existence annoys him greatly, though he always plays the doting nephew when he visits. I imagine he hopes I have saved a great deal of my allowance and will leave it to him in my will. Between you and me, aside from small pensions for Humphry and Mrs James, the only person who gets anything from my will is Elijah. The bulk is going to the Battersea Dogs' Home."

"I completely approve. The dogs will be much more grateful."

"Quite! And, as far as I know, they don't wish me dead!" Miss Sampford's humour had grown morbid, "This last year I have heard William Henry is truly struggling to keep the estate financially viable. He had invested quite heavily in factories producing war goods, which provided him with a considerable fortune during those terrible years, but he failed to see the writing on the wall and pull out early enough. When the war ended and the factories went bust, so did he. I hear he spent most of his war fortune writing off debts. I don't know if he will be able to keep the estate. My allowance is tied up in several investments specifically set up by father on John's advice. Not only is it safe from the misfortunes of the estate, but William Henry can't touch the capital until I am dead and in my grave. Can you see why he might be motivated to encourage my demise?"

"If you were to be scared to death, by a ghost say, no one could deem it murder." Clara understood.

"Precisely. In any case, old lady's die all the time from their hearts failing, who is to say if it had a little help from a spectre?"

Clara nodded and sat back in her chair musing on the problem. Between the greedy Mr Mollinson and the avaricious William Henry there was motive enough to perpetrate a crime, whether that was scaring an old lady out of her home, or to her death.

"Clara, you really must solve this before any harm comes to me." Miss Sampford suddenly sounded very frail, her pluck and strength had abruptly drained away.

"Miss Sampford, I shall not allow any harm to befall you." Clara swore, turning to the old woman and taking her hand.

Miss Sampford squeezed her fingers around Clara's.

"I have been so scared." She said, a tremble in her voice.

"Well, I take no nonsense from the living or the dead, so no more fears. I shall have this solved before Christmas is out."

Miss Sampford smiled.

"I am so jolly glad you came."

Chapter Six

"And what does this do?" Oliver Bankes picked up a box that appeared to contain a pencil poised on a wire over a sheet of paper.

"Really Mr Bankes, would you mind not touching?" Andrews snatched the box from his hands, "It's a vibration detector. Self-built. When I wind it up and set it going the paper will slowly scroll through, the hours are marked on the paper. If something, say footsteps, causes a vibration near the device the pencil moves and draws on the paper. I can then see at what time the vibrations were caused and the duration. See, your moving of the box has caused it to draw here?"

Oliver noted a faint mark on the paper.

"Do ghosts cause vibrations?"

"That is one of the questions I am trying to answer. Here, just hold this." Andrews dumped a large ball of fishing twine into Oliver's hands in the vain hope this might stop him from touching anything else.

"What about the flour we sprinkled on the back stairs?"

"To detect footprints. The servants have been instructed to use the main stairs; therefore any footprints that appear in the flour are clearly supernatural."

"Or made by an intruder?"

Andrews gave a grumpy sigh.

"That too." He conceded.

He stretched the fishing twine across the threshold of the open library door.

"Is that to trip a ghost?" Oliver asked.

"No, Mr Bankes, merely to demonstrate if any physical being has entered the room." Andrews said with tetchy patience, "Now, if you would just turn off the wall lamps I would like to observe the hallway in darkness."

Oliver obeyed and the corridor went pitch black. There was silence. As Oliver's eyes adjusted to the dim light he slowly made out the doorways along either side of the hall and the thin bars of light creeping from under them.

"Interesting isn't it Mr Bankes? With all the doors closed the hall is almost without light and would be challenging to negotiate." Andrews lit a bull's-eye lantern he had carried upstairs and shone its bright beam over the walls, "I look for cracks in the walls which might allow sound to travel from next door. Or any other natural means for the phenomena."

Andrews started up the hall. Oliver crept behind him.

"Have you ever taken a photograph of a ghost?" Oliver said, reaching out one hand to feel the wall and keep his balance.

"No. I don't think it is possible." Andrews snapped, he was shining the lantern at the door to the back stairs.

"I brought my camera to try and take a picture of the ghost." Oliver replied mildly.

Andrews paused.

"You have a camera?"

"Yes."

"A good one?"

"I am a photographer by profession." Oliver chuckled.

Andrews turned slowly, blinding Oliver with lamplight.

"Could we rig your camera to go off when someone walked into one of my wires?"

Oliver gave it some thought.

"Probably."

Andrews shut down the lamp and the world fell into darkness. Then he snapped on a wall lamp and Oliver blinked furiously as he tried to restore his vision.

"Let's try it. Fetch your camera. If, as your friend Miss Fitzgerald insists, this ghost is of flesh and blood, why don't we set a trap?"

It was almost midnight by the time Clara went up to bed. Miss Sampford had gone a little ahead of her, after much reminiscing about her suffrage days. Clara had gone to check on Tommy before mounting the stairs. She was confronted in the second floor corridor by a web of wires and contraptions. She stared at it all for a moment before moving a step forward and causing a bell to ring. Oliver and Andrews both appeared from their rooms in an instant.

"Do be careful Miss Fitzgerald!" Andrews rebuked Clara, "I have already had to tell Miss Sampford about ringing my bell unnecessarily."

"What is all this?" Clara gestured to Andrews' gadgets.

"Tests for the ghost." Oliver said calmly, coming forward into the hall, "Here, I'll show you the safe passage through."

He helped Clara to avoid setting off anymore wires in the approach to her room. She felt as though she was performing some strange dance as she tiptoed around small boxes, dodged tripwires and squeezed around Oliver's camera. When she reached the door of her room she looked back at the maze she had just negotiated.

"I can only hope our ghost is light on his or her feet, else we will all be disturbed by the commotion."

"I would expect such cynicism off a sceptic." Andrews snorted, "How many ghosts have you encountered before, may I ask?"

"I may safely say, none."

"Precisely, so do not impugn my methods. I have been doing this for twenty years and I have seen things that would have you screaming for your mother."

"Really?" Clara said archly raising one eyebrow, "I am not inclined towards screaming."

"Maybe after tonight you will be." Andrews said firmly.

Clara merely smiled.

"We shall see. Good night all, the witching hour is nearly upon us and I would not wish to deter our ghost by staying up too late." Clara gave a nod to Oliver and then entered her bedroom.

There was a fire crackling in the grate and a hot water bottle in the bed. Annie was sitting in her dressing gown on a stool before the fire, a Bible in one hand and a large spoon in the other.

"The Bible I can understand." Clara said as she flopped down onto the bed, "But the spoon?"

"It's silver, biggest bit of silver Mrs James had. I promised on my life I would bring it back safe in the morning. You ward off all manner of supernatural evils with silver, it's well-known." Annie looked at the spoon she held poised upright in her hand, "Actually it's silver plated, but I think that still counts."

"Are you anticipating the ghost coming after us in our beds?" Clara asked as seriously as she could manage, the image of Annie brandishing a silver spoon with such a determined look on her face was almost too much to bear.

"I ain't taking any chances." Annie said staunchly.

"And do you intend to sit on that stool all night?"

"No." Annie reluctantly admitted, "I was just waiting for you."

"Go to bed now Annie, I'll guard the door." Clara assured her, "And don't be afraid of ghosts, all of this can be explained by some purely natural cause."

"Yes, but Flo told me about the grave the workers came across at the bottom of the garden!"

"I know, but that is just a rumour. Anyway, as a good Christian you should be comforted by the knowledge that spirits don't remain forever stuck in their graves, but go up to Heaven or down to Hell, depending on their moral outlook. So there can't possibly be such a thing as ghosts."

The spoon sagged in Annie's hand.

"That is true." She said thoughtfully, "Reverend Bates says the spirit departs within the first hour of death."

"Well, there you go."

"But then why do people say they have seen ghosts?"

"Oh, for lots of reasons." Clara shrugged, "For attention, for mischief or just because they have mistaken something natural for a ghost."

Annie considered this a while longer.

"All right then, I'll go to bed. But shout if you need anything."

"I will indeed."

Annie went off to the dressing room and lightly pulled the door to. Clara rested a moment then rose and dragged off her clothes, sleep already summoning her. She drew on a nightgown, turned off the light and slipped under the bed covers, resting her feet on the warm stone of the hot water bottle. It was not long before she had drifted off.

It must have been around two o'clock she heard a bell ring distantly. It was too soft a sound to truly rouse her from sleep, but then there was a crash, a burst of light and a loud thud. Clara sprang from her bed, just as Annie came racing through from the dressing room.

"What is it?" The maid cried.

"Go grab your spoon." Clara said in jest and Annie raced off.

Clara rolled her eyes, reprimanding herself for being so flippant. Then she grabbed her dressing gown and hurried out into the hall. She found Oliver leaning over the prone figure of Elijah Sampford, while Miss Sampford peered out from her doorway. Mr Andrews was looking even grumpier than normal, having had to fight his way past Oliver's camera which had fallen in front of his door. Clara stared around the hallway; there was no sign of a ghost.

"What happened?" She came up behind Oliver.

"Mr Sampford set off everything!" Andrews yelled, pointing a finger at Elijah on the floor.

"I thought I heard a bell." Elijah groaned, rubbing his head, his feet were still tangled in fishing wire, "I came out to see what it was and I stumbled in the dark, then there was this flash…"

"He set off my camera." Oliver explained, "Unfortunately he also fell over it and smashed the glass plate."

"Why didn't you stay in your room as instructed?" Andrews cried out in frustration.

"I heard a bell." Elijah repeated weakly.

"Actually, I heard a bell too." Clara intervened.

Andrews was distracted from his tirade.

"Roughly Miss Fitzgerald, which direction did the sound come from? To the left of your room or to the right?" He asked.

Clara had to think about this as the noise had been barely noticeable and she would have discarded it for a dream, had Elijah not heard it also.

"I suppose, it seemed to come from the left of my room."

"Would you concur with that Mr Sampford?"

Elijah had sat up and was in the process of untangling his slippers from the fishing line.

"Yes, I think that is fair to say." He looked up.

"I set a bell by the back stairs." Andrews spryly leapt over Elijah and headed for the door at the end of the corridor.

He pulled open the door and peered onto the staircase.

"Footprints!"

Clara hurried to join him, followed by Oliver.

"So we have had a living intruder!" Clara declared.

"Not necessarily Miss Fitzgerald! Your ignorance shows yet again!" Andrews was most gleeful, "It is a known fact that ghosts can leave footprints! Look how they seem to begin just here, as if the spirit came from downstairs. Yet we know everyone was upstairs!"

"But you can't deny a person could have made these prints just as easily." Clara argued.

"And how did they get in?" Andrews snapped back.

"I haven't determined that yet."

"You are clutching at straws, Miss Fitzgerald, just because you refuse to believe in ghosts!"

"And you refuse to accept what is before your eyes. Living people make footprints and ring bells!"

"Then why did Mr Sampford not catch this living ghost?" Andrews demanded.

"Who knows how long it took him to climb out of his bed, don a dressing gown and dash out here. A living intruder would very likely have bolted as soon as they heard the bell. For that matter, why did he not see a spirit, if that is what caused the noise? Surely a spectre would not be perturbed at the sound of a bell?"

"Actually," Elijah broke into the argument, his grin slowly returning even if his head did pound, "I think I did see something."

"Why didn't you say before?" Andrews jumped back towards the lad, "What did you see?"

"Well the hall was rather dark and I hadn't switched on any lights, but in the moment I triggered the camera and the flash went off, I was looking to my left and in the flare of light I thought I saw a cloaked figure."

"Which then vanished!" Andrews declared triumphantly.

"Or ran up the stairs." Clara replied.

"Then why don't we interview the servants and see if any of them were prowling about?" Andrews was quite belligerent by now, "But first I want Mr Bankes to take a photograph of those footprints."

"At least on that I concur, they are evidence."

Andrews gave Clara a scowl. Twenty minutes later the pair had tramped up to the attic and disturbed the servants from their slumber. Miss Sampford was not pleased about the matter as she didn't need her cook or maids further spooked. But Andrews had insisted and Clara had to agree; the sooner it was clarified that none of the servants had gone downstairs, the sooner they could get on with looking for the real criminal.

Around half past two in the morning Mrs James and the two maids were all gathered into Mr Humphry's room for an interview. Mr Humphry happened to have the biggest sleeping quarters and it seemed appropriate, as he was the head of the servants, that it should be his room in which the matter was dealt with. Clara started the conversation.

"There has been quite a commotion downstairs. Now, we just want to know if anyone has been past the second floor using the back stairs in the last few hours."

"Is Miss Sampford all right?" Mrs James asked instantly.

"She is fine. Mr Sampford heard something and tripped over a camera when investigating." Clara avoided details.

"Heard something?" Mrs James went pale, "The ghost?"

"If Mr Sampford had not smashed the camera we might have been able to tell." Andrews said gruffly, "Now, can you answer the question?"

"I haven't left my bed." Mrs James assured them, "Does Mr Sampford need anything? Is he hurt?"

"Only his pride." Andrews grumbled, "What about you?"

He pointed a finger at Flo.

"I never leave my room at night, just in case." She said immediately.

"And you?" The pointing finger turned on Jane.

The girl, a little younger than Flo, was trembling slightly.

"If someone went downstairs," She said in a quavering voice, "Would they be in a lot of trouble?"

Before Andrews spoke, Clara butted in.

"Absolutely not. No one was banned from going downstairs. We only want to know if what Mr Sampford heard was an actual person. There nothing to be concerned about."

"And," Jane's voice had almost dropped to a squeaky whisper, "And, if that person accidentally forgot to not use the back stairs, would they be in trouble for that?"

"No." Clara said gently, "Jane, did you go downstairs?"

Jane gave a little sniff.

"I wanted a drink of water, that's all. I remembered to use the main stairs to go down, but when I went to come up I forgot myself and just ran up the back stairs. It was about an hour ago, I suppose."

Andrews was about to explode with indignation, so Clara shoved him firmly out of the room.

"Thank you Jane, you did nothing wrong. Go back to bed." She said as she disappeared after him.

She only just managed to get Andrews onto the main stairs before his temper let loose.

"That damn stupid child ruined everything!" He snarled.

"These things happen Mr Andrews, at least we have explained the footprints."

"You are just delighted to be right." Andrews pointed that aggressive finger at her, "Hah, but I have the last laugh Miss Fitzgerald, for what about the bell? Who rang that I ask you?"

"Could not someone going up the stairs have done it?" Clara suggested.

"No, no, no. I have you there! Something rang that bell and you can't prove it was a person." Andrews gave her a smug smile and then trotted off down the stairs.

Clara found herself screwing up her hands into fists. Some people, she found herself thinking, were completely unbearable.

Chapter Seven

Clara found Tommy in his bedroom wrapped up to the chin in a thick coat and scarf and sniffling loudly. He sneezed into a handkerchief as she entered.

"How are you?" She asked.

"Dying." He snuffled miserably.

"Jolly good. I was thinking you could pay a call on the British library and see what material they have on the history of Berkeley Square." Clara said, having not listened to Tommy's answer.

Her brother glared at her over his scarf. Clara paused for a moment.

"Unless you don't feel up to it?"

"I did say I was dying."

"Sorry, I wasn't listening."

Tommy sighed.

"That fellow Andrews really has you in a tizzy, doesn't he?"

"He is impossible!" Clara said rather loudly, then she looked guiltily at the open door. She went and closed it before, in a more subdued tone, she continued, "He refuses to listen to rational thinking."

"I heard the commotion last night. I feel quite left out down here." Tommy sniffed morosely.

"Quite frankly, you are better off down here. He has turned the second floor hallway into a spider's web of wires and managed to give poor Elijah a mild concussion in the process. He has bells and things that measure vibrations. You should have seen his face when he thought he had caught ghostly footprints in the flour he left on the staircase. He almost exploded when he learned one of the maids had accidentally made them."

"So, no phantom last night?"

"As far as I can tell…" Clara hesitated, "Look, between you and me Tommy, I can account for everything that went on up there except for the ringing of a bell. Mr Andrews is adamant the bell would not have rung just because a maid ran up the back stairs. Naturally I didn't believe him, so I conducted an experiment while everyone was at breakfast. I ran up and down the stairs several times and the bell remained silent. The only time I caused it to ring was when I actually plucked the wire it is connected to. Now I heard that bell ring in the night and Elijah says the same, of course he could be lying or mistaken, perhaps he tripped the bell himself. But why would he be out in the hallway in the middle of the night?"

"So something could have been abroad last night?"

"Or someone." Clara pulled up a chair next to her brother and sat down, "Unfortunately Miss Sampford is in a position where at least two people find her continued existence troublesome. She masks it well, but she is very scared. If someone is trying to frighten her to death they are doing a jolly good job."

"People play some nasty games."

"Don't they just. Look I am going to pay a few calls before Miss Sampford's relatives arrive, and Andrews has some extra ghost hunters turning up to help him conduct an all-night vigil. Do you want anything before I go?"

"No, only a damn end to this cold."

"Never mind, it will be better soon." Clara stood and kissed him on the forehead, "See if you can keep Oliver

61

out of trouble, will you? He has become rather taken with this ghost hunting lark and is following Andrews everywhere."

"If he happens to appear on the ground floor, I'll nab him." Tommy promised.

Clara headed out into the Square. The morning was brisk, a hint of snow in the sky. Everyone was wrapped up as tightly as they could be in coats, hats and gloves. Clara settled a scarf about her neck and headed towards number 49. She knocked on the door and waited to see if anyone was in. There was silence.

"Right Mr Mollinson, where am I likely to find you?"

Luckily Mollinson had left his business card with Miss Sampford on each occasion he visited and Clara had taken care to collect one of these cards before leaving the house. She read off his office address then went to find the nearest tube station.

Clara had travelled via London's great underground network of trains only once before. The great labyrinth of tunnels, all tiled in white and with the smooth gliding carriages running on electric rails, filled her with a sense of awe. It seemed remarkable that anyone could create such a magnificent subterranean world and, to think, some parts of the system were nearly sixty years old already. On her first visit she had been around twelve and it was part of a school outing to see a pantomime at Christmas. The girls had been allowed to buy their own tickets, which seemed at the time extremely grown-up. Going on the trains, however, had been quite daunting for some of them and one girl became overcome with claustrophobia. Not even the headmistress' usually infallible smelling salts could bring her out of it. For Clara the journey had been an exciting adventure, something which the pantomime, their ultimate destination, could hardly compete with. Clara felt a thrill of elation as the train shot down the tunnels, electric lights on the walls bursting in and out of her vision. She felt like a mole burying underground and it was with a strange pang of giddiness that she wondered at how fast they were going and whether the train could brake quickly enough in an emergency, say like a cave-in of the roof. On reflection, Clara's musings in this direction (unfortunately voiced out-loud) had probably not helped the claustrophobic girl's panic.

Over a decade on, Clara bought her ticket without thinking and boarded a carriage with a sense of purpose rather than excitement. She took a seat among businessmen, office girls and casual shoppers, wondering if her old school still ran trips to the pantomime at Christmas. The carriage was cold, not something Clara had remembered, and the passengers were all engaged in their own activities, mostly reading newspapers or looking out the windows. No one seemed inclined to speak and Clara found herself regretting she had not picked up a newspaper before boarding. Somehow the novel glow of tube travel, which she had carried with her all these years, now seemed faded. She was rather relieved when she reached her stop and headed out into the street.

Almost at once Clara found herself immersed in a crowd of Christmas shoppers. There was hardly a gap to walk through on the busy pavements as people nipped between shops, grabbed tables in restaurants and cafes, or wasted time before the theatres opened. People were smoking feverishly, partly to pass the time and partly to warm themselves. Clara found herself walking through a fog of smoke that hung just at head level.

She stepped off the pavement briefly, thinking to dodge around the hordes, and was almost flattened by an omnibus. She jumped back onto the pavement as the driver shook his fist at her and told her to be more careful. Now Clara was paying attention she realised the roads were far busier than she was used to in Brighton. Some form of vehicle came past almost every moment. Despite this people were crossing the road, dodging cars without any apparent concern for their wellbeing. Clara nudged her way back onto the pavement and made sure to stay close to the shops rather than risk being knocked into the thoroughfare.

It was slow progress up the street, pushing through the people and constantly repeating 'excuse me', 'may I?' 'would you mind?' all the time. Clara treated herself to a bag of roast chestnuts off a street seller to warm her hands. Finally, after what seemed a considerable age of bumping into people, Clara found the office building belonging to Mr Mollinson. There was a brass plaque on the wall bearing his name. She entered the foyer and found herself before a concierge.

"Is Mr Mollinson in his office?"

"Have you an appointment?" The concierge, a young man with greased hair, asked.

"No, I have only just come down to London and was hoping he might be free to see me."

"Mr Mollinson rarely speaks to people without an appointment." The concierge continued in a rather grave tone.

Clara felt he was rather over-stepping the limitations of his role.

"Might you at least try contacting him? And if he is not available today, then perhaps we could arrange a more convenient time?"

The concierge gave himself a moment to consider the acceptability of this request.

"I suppose so." He picked up the receiver of a large black phone and dialled a number, "Hello? Mr Mollinson? It is Patrickson at the front desk. A lady is requesting to speak with you." The concierge paused to listen, "He wishes to know what the matter is concerning."

"Please could you say it is Miss Fitzgerald wishing to speak to him on Miss Sampford's behalf?"

The concierge repeated the message, then again paused to receive instructions. His face slowly took on a look of surprise. He carefully put down the receiver.

"Mr Mollinson says he will see you at once." He said, clearly astonished, "Please go to the third floor, first door on your left."

Clara was not surprised at Mollinson's willingness, not once he had heard the name of Miss Sampford. In fact, his sudden interest only helped fix in Clara's mind his potential as a suspect. He was clearly still very keen to get his hands on number 50. But keen enough to frighten a little old lady into abandoning her home? Now that really was the question.

Clara ascended the stairs, which curved upwards in a wide spiral, wondering how long an audience she would have with Mollinson once he learned she was not there to help arrange the sale of the house. She found his office – marked with his name – easily enough and knocked. A male voice asked her to enter.

Mollinson was sat behind a large mahogany desk; it was an antique, once owned by his grandfather. Mollinson valued its origins as much as the statement it made to people entering his office. Mollinson was all about statements. Everything he wore, every piece of furniture in his office, everything he did, even down to the pen he used to write with, was all about drawing attention and displaying his power and wealth. When he sat behind his desk he wanted people to see a man of quality, dressed in an expensive tailored suit. He wore his hair slightly longer than most to make him appear younger and was vain enough to have it dyed to mask most of the grey. He was pleased that his face did not require similar treatment, though he had been known to surreptitiously use his wife's wrinkle cream before going to bed. He kept out of the sun, got enough sleep and always used a sharp razor when shaving to avoid cuts. If his skin was not exactly flawless, it was at least well-tended, he was satisfied that he did not look his fifty-five years and had not suffered the ravages of time so many of his business fellows had.

As he sat at his desk, toying with an ivory letter-opener, he was arrogant enough to believe he could charm anybody into doing anything he wished. And now he believed those charms had worked their magic on Miss Sampford and had finally convinced her to sell.

He rose as Clara entered and smile broadly.

"Do take a seat Miss Fitzgerald."

Clara sat in front of the desk, noting astutely that her chair was a fraction lower than Mollinson's, so he appeared to tower over her slightly. It was a neat psychological trick she had heard about before.

"Good morning, Mr Mollinson. Is it always so busy in the streets around here?"

"Well it is Christmas." Mollinson lounged back in his chair, "How can I help you? You mentioned Miss Sampford?"

"Yes, I am working on her behalf."

"And how much is she willing to accept for number 50?" Mollinson pulled a cheque-book from a drawer as he spoke and held his pen poised over it.

"You mistake my intent. Miss Sampford is not interested in selling number 50."

"Still?" Mollinson's façade of charm momentarily deserted him, "I thought she would have come around by now."

"Is there any particular reason for that Mr Mollinson?"

The businessman gave her a puzzled look.

"What do you mean?"

"You implied you have been expecting her to 'come around' to the idea of selling her home. Could you say why you were so certain she would?"

"No." Mollinson looked worried.

"You have heard about Miss Sampford's problems?"

"Problems?"

"The ghost." Clara elaborated, feeling a touch exasperated by the man, "You commented on the problem to her."

"Oh that. Does she still have a ghost?"

"Yes Mr Mollinson, perhaps you know something about it?"

Mollinson took a moment to grasp her insinuation.

"Miss Fitzgerald, who exactly are you?" He demanded to know.

Clara calmly fished a card out of her bag and handed it to him.

"A private detective? But you're a woman..." Mollinson bit his tongue, "I see where this is going, I'm not stupid. You want to know if I have been trying to scare an old lady out of her home, well the answer is a firm no."

"You have to admit, if this haunting forces Miss Sampford to move, it will be very advantageous for you." Clara pointed out.

"That's by the by. I don't go around scaring people. What sort of man do you think I am?"

"You can't deny Miss Sampford's refusal to sell has been a nuisance."

"Every project I do has a thousand nuisances. I work around them to find a solution. In this case I made an offer to the landlord of number 48, he accepted and now I have my two buildings for my hotel."

"So why do you still want number 50?"

"Aesthetics mainly. You see number 50 and number 49 are laid out on very similar plans and have identical frontages, which would make combining them a lot simpler. Number 48 will take more work, but that inconvenience is not enough to make me consider scaring Miss Sampford out of her home." Mr Mollinson sat back in his chair. Clara had to admit his arguments were quite convincing.

"Might I ask, do you have men working in number 49?"

"On and off. Until I knew where I stood with number 50 I could only do so much. They have been stripping off the old wallpaper and moving some of the doorways. I also need to look into the electrical arrangements, this is going to be an upmarket hotel you understand. I want electric lighting and hot water in every room. That means plumbers and electricians."

"I don't suppose they ever work late?"

"No. Are you imagining one of my men might be masquerading as a ghost?"

"Only by accident. Quite frankly Mr Mollinson I don't believe in spirits and I aim to find a logical and very living cause for the disturbances at Miss Sampford's home."

"Well just don't look at me. I have nothing to do with it. Now, if you don't mind I have a lot of work to do."

"Thank you for your time Mr Mollinson, might I ask one last thing?"

Mollinson gave her a suspicious look, but didn't say she couldn't.

"Might I borrow a key for number 49?"

"Why?" Mollinson asked gruffly.

"I just want to take a look around and see if there is any possibility of someone making noise in that building which could transmit to number 50."

"I'm not the cause of this 'ghost'." Mollinson snapped.

"I don't mean to imply you are, but if someone wanted to create a supposed ghost and knew a house was sitting empty, they might be tempted to sneak in and cause mischief."

"I'll think about it." Mollinson said, with the implication that he would not.

Clara decided she would be best to leave while she was ahead.

"Thank you for your time Mr Mollinson." She made her way downstairs and back into the heaving throng of Christmas shoppers outside.

Chapter Eight

It took far longer than Clara liked to get back to Berkeley Square and the afternoon was wearing thin by the time she was in the front door. She gave her hat and coat to Mr Humphry and went immediately to see Tommy. She was pleased to find he had a blisteringly hot fire burning in the hearth of his room and went straight to it to warm her hands.

"Cold out there?" Tommy asked, he had removed one scarf so Clara assumed he was beginning to feel better.

"Bitter." She answered, "Mollinson proved a dead end, so far. What are you reading?"

Tommy held up the blue bound book he was perusing.

"Carnacki the Ghost Finder. Andrews loaned it to me. Actually, he loaned it to Oliver, but such is the way of things." Tommy grinned.

"And what does Carnacki make of ghosts?"

"Pretty cynical, much like you. Tends to find they are the product of some nefarious human being rather than anything supernatural, though he has encountered the odd real one. Its fiction, you understand."

Clara nodded as she rubbed her hands together.

"Anything exciting happen while I was gone?"

"Annie says Jane is threatening to leave."

"Oh dear."

"She has convinced her otherwise. Think it was largely to do with being accosted by that ghastly ghost hunter in the middle of the night. Talking of which, his troops have arrived."

"Oh really." Clara considered this, "What are they like?"

"One is a tall fellow called Simon Jones, about thirty-five, looks like an academic or something. Dreadfully enthusiastic and talks a lot, quite gives you a headache. Then there is a woman called Bridget Harper, can't quite work her out. She seems rather aloof and rather sad. She didn't say much when she arrived. Looks about the same age as Jones. And lastly there is Captain Adams, ex-army, looks about seventy. Typical former soldier type; brusque, overbearing and with a moustache a walrus would be proud of."

Clara laughed gently.

"So, have we much to fear from them?"

"I doubt it, though Adams has brought a pistol and a shotgun. Apparently he takes ghost hunting quite literally."

"That's not good, poor Miss Sampford. I hope she doesn't find her wallpaper smattered with holes."

"Let's just hope that ghost really is an incorporeal being, or else the wallpaper may be smattered with a lot worse."

"Indeed."

"Now to Miss Sampford's relations. William Henry Sampford and the, ahem, delightful Amelia Sampford arrived roughly an hour ago. I was introduced as a friend of Elijah's. I have to say Miss Sampford seemed quite in a dither around them."

"Tell me about them, as much as you can." Clara settled herself on the edge of Tommy's bed and prepared to listen.

"My first impression was a bit like that of Captain Adams. William Henry seemed rather abrupt and fierce, the sort of man who always gets his own way. His disdain for Miss Sampford was apparent at once. I didn't talk to him for long, but I got the impression that he has a cruel streak about him and has very little concern for anyone else. He gave my legs a funny look, perhaps he thinks I took to a wheelchair for pleasure." There was a sour note in Tommy's words, "His wife was little better. She flapped around Miss Sampford, but it was all so false. Kisses on the cheek and light hugs, so insincere. I spotted her eyeing up the room as soon as Miss Sampford was distracted, no doubt taking a look at how her husband's money was being spent. Mr Andrews walked in about then and that didn't go down well at all. Miss Sampford tried to avoid explaining his presence, but Andrews let it slip. I imagine the looks that came across William Henry's and Amelia's faces would be akin to if they had stepped in a recent deposit of horse dung with their best shoes. I think the only thing that saved Andrews was that Miss Sampford said he had come by Elijah's request. It seems William Henry is rather more indulgent to his cousin, probably because he doesn't have to fund his existence."

"William Henry is not a believer in ghosts then?"

"Apparently not. He sneered the whole time Miss Sampford was explaining the situation. I almost could see him wondering if he could have her locked away in an asylum for suggesting her house was haunted."

"We need to watch him. That could be just what he planned. Use the ghost he had created to prove Miss Sampford had lost her marbles."

"I would watch that Amelia even closer." Tommy said, "There was something about her I didn't like. The sort of woman you could imagine drowning kittens and enjoying it."

Clara grimaced at the analogy.

"Anything else?"

"The Sampfords are sleeping on the third floor, out of harm's way. I thought you would be glad about that."

"I am, in a way. But it might have been just as advisable to have had them in close quarters where they could be watched. I fancy setting one of those bells Mr Andrews has outside their door, to see if they like to roam about in the night."

"Even if they are behind the ghost, and certainly I would not put it past those two heartless creatures, they could not be acting in person. They must have hired someone."

"Yes, I quite agree with that." Clara wondered how one went about hiring a person to play a ghost.

It was then that the doorbell rang. Both Tommy and Clara looked up.

"More guests?" Said Clara.

"Seems likely." Tommy answered.

Clara stood and headed for the doorway. She had to leave Tommy's room and walk down a short corridor to see around the staircase and to the front door. As she stood partly in the shadows, she saw Humphry open the door to an elderly couple.

"Mr and Mrs Sampford." She heard Humphry intone, "How lovely to see you again."

"London doesn't get any better Humphry." The elderly gentleman puttered as he came into the hall and deposited his umbrella and hat in the butler's waiting arms, "Has my nephew and his awful wife arrived yet?"

"Edward!" Hissed the woman beside him.

"Well they are awful Hilda. You can't deny that."

Miss Sampford suddenly appeared from the drawing room. For once she seemed delighted to have guests.

"Edward!" She flung her arms around the old man.

"Hello sis, are you keeping well?"

Clara decided it was time to make her presence known and to discover exactly which members of the Sampford clan the new arrivals were. She walked out into the hall as if she had just come from the far room.

"Oh Clara, this is my dear brother Edward and his lovely wife Hilda." Miss Sampford announced with a smile, "Edward, would you believe, is ten years older than me, but he doesn't look it, does he?"

Clara came forward and politely shook Edward's hand.

"This is my friend from Brighton, Miss Clara Fitzgerald. I knew her mother." Miss Sampford continued, "She has come to stay for Christmas with her brother Thomas Fitzgerald, a war hero you know."

Clara found Miss Sampford's lies strangely disturbing as well as flattering. She shook Hilda's hand and the older woman peered at her short-sightedly through narrow glasses.

"Nice to meet you Miss Fitzgerald. It will be lovely to have a younger person at the dinner table, other than Elijah of course." Hilda was a warm sort of person, one you could imagine hugging comfortably. Her head and hands shook constantly as she spoke, as if they had a life of her own. It was quite distracting.

"Edward and Hilda complete our Christmas party." Miss Sampford informed Clara with a steady look, "I suggest we all freshen up before dinner. Edward, I have had Mrs James cook your favourite boiled gammon with cider gravy."

Edward beamed brightly.

"Hear that Hilda? Cider gravy."

Hilda rolled her eyes in mock opprobrium.

"Humphry will show you to your rooms. Clara might I speak with you for a moment?" Miss Sampford retreated to the drawing room and Clara followed as Edward and Hilda Sampford were shown upstairs.

"Shut the door Clara."

Clara obeyed then noted that Miss Sampford had poured herself a large glass of whisky.

"My nephew has arrived." She took a long drink, "Did you know?"

"Tommy told me."

"Poor Tommy, why am I related to such dreadful people? William Henry is such a blunderbuss."

"Miss Sampford, you may have asked me down here to investigate a ghost, but that doesn't mean you can't rely on my help in other ways." Clara went and sat next to her client and touched her arm lightly.

"You are most kind, dear. All that business last night has quite shaken me."

"Well it mustn't. Last night was nothing more than human clumsiness and a lot of silliness." Clara smiled, "I hear Mr Andrews did not find favour with your nephew?"

"Hmph. William Henry will tolerate Andrews, but only because Elijah's father was very generous towards him in the past and he doesn't dare offend the boy. For William, being nice to people is only worth it if money is involved."

"Are Elijah's parents coming down?"

"No, Elijah's father is deceased and his mother is quite frail these days, so she remains in the country all year round." Miss Sampford took more whisky, "I just have this feeling in my bones that this will be an awful Christmas."

"Nonsense." Clara said reassuringly, "Everything will be fine. It is the anxiety of these last few weeks playing on your nerves."

"I hope you are right Clara."

"Really now, what bad thing could possibly happen?"

Miss Sampford's face took on a sad expression.

"That is not a question you should ask when you are discussing the Sampford family."

Chapter Nine

Annie helped Jane peel potatoes. The girl looked utterly despondent and had sobbed for most of the morning. She was mortified she had forgotten Miss Sampford's instructions and run up the back stairs last night, and she was terrified of bumping into Mr Andrews. The arrival of further guests had not eased her concerns.

"If you girls are done with that, you can go sweep the flour off the back stairs." Mrs James was fussing over several boiling pans and rapidly losing patience with a sherry trifle that was refusing to set, "Go on Jane, take the dustpan and brush. Annie will keep you company."

Annie found it mildly amusing how quickly she had been accepted into the household, it was as if she had always been there and certainly Mrs James had no concerns about asking her to undertake chores with the other maids. Had the situation been different Annie might have been mildly offended but, as it stood, she was well aware of the advantage to be had in being seen as part of the staff. She followed Jane to the back stairs.

"I shouldn't say, but look at this mess." Jane motioned to several sets of floury footsteps dotting the stairs. What with Andrews analysing the scene, followed by his troop of ghost hunters and the servants clattering up and down the stairs, the flour had been scattered everywhere.

"I'll fetch a damp cloth." Said Annie.

She disappeared briefly and returned with a bucket and a clean rag. While Jane swept up the worst of the mess, Annie washed down the stairs.

"Is there not a light in here, it's so dark." Annie protested as they worked their way upwards.

"No, I should have brought a candle." Jane swept at a pile of flour near the skirting board, "Shall I fetch one."

She looked to her companion but Annie had paused and was staring at the shut door to their right. They were just at the third floor, collecting the flour that had been traipsed up the stairs. There were people talking in the corridor. Jane opened her mouth to say something, but Annie signalled for silence. The two maids stood still and listened.

"Really William you must do something!"

"And what exactly do you propose?"

"I swear that was a new rug downstairs and two maids? What is the woman thinking? Quite frankly, I can't see why she needs the butler."

"Humphry is an institution. He used to work for father."

"May I point out that we don't have a butler? Really William, she is just frittering away our money."

"What do you expect me to do, bump the old girl off?"

There was a long silence.

"Amelia!"

"Well, she is old. Who would notice?"

"I'm doing everything that I can and that's an end to it."

"Clearly it is not enough."

"I don't intend to murder my own aunt."

"Then what are you up to? Don't deny that you have been doing something. All those secret trips to London. Perhaps murder isn't on your mind, but you are plotting something."

"Do be quiet Amelia."

"All this talk of ghosts. What is that about? Has the old girl lost her mind?"

Again there was silence.

"William?"

"I don't want to talk about it anymore."

"You're up to something, I know you are up to something."

A door opened and then closed. Footsteps retreated down the corridor. Annie glanced at Jane. The girl was shaking.

"My poor mistress." She moaned softly.

Annie dropped her wet cloth into the bucket. She needed to speak with Clara as soon as she could.

~~*~~

Clara had taken the opportunity, while wandering around London, to do a bit of Christmas shopping and she wanted to carefully stash away her gifts in her bedroom. This, however, was proving problematic, for Mr Andrews and his band of ghost hunters were stationed in the corridor plotting out their next move. Oliver was hovering nearby with his camera.

"The only way to solve this one Andrews is to lock every bally door and keep an eye on the entire floor!" A surly man with a huge moustache was declaring to the group. Clara assumed this was Captain Adams.

"Not all the doors can be locked." Andrews said mildly, his usual gruffness had been tempered by the presence of the military man.

"What rot! Then I'll stand here with my shotgun and shoot the first soul who comes through that door!" The captain waved an arm at the doorway to the back stairs.

"Really Adams, you may take out an unfortunate maid." A woman, Clara imagined this must be Bridget Harper, told the captain sternly. She was leaning in a languid manner against the wall and looked a tad dazed, as if she was not entirely present in spirit and mind.

"Have you tried a pentangle? I was reading they can be quite useful against this sort of thing." The final member of the party (it had to be Simon Jones, Clara concluded) piped up. He was a tall, lean man with a slight stoop, carrying a book under his arm, "I've always wanted to try one of those."

"I told you before, none of this black magic nonsense." Captain Adams barked.

"It's not black magic, it can be used for protection, really captain…"

"Gentlemen, we do things scientifically." Andrews calmed the argument, "We will set out the bells and wires again. We will put a wax seal around the door too, to see if it has to be opened to allow the ghost through. All the guests will be informed to stay in their rooms. We will take turns to keep a vigil. Now Bridget, when will you feel up to performing?"

The woman looked at him with a strangely unfocused expression.

"Who is that woman?" She pointed to Clara.

"Miss Clara Fitzgerald." Andrews said through gritted teeth, "Might I introduce my associates Captain Adams, Simon Jones and Mrs Bridget Harper."

Bridget pushed herself away from the wall and walked towards Clara. She had strange, hazy blue eyes that made her seem to look straight through you.

"You walk with the dead." She told Clara solemnly.

Clara imagined this was a scare-tactic and took no notice.

"Might I ask," She said looking past Bridget to Andrews, "What is the point of tripwires if you then complain when a person, such as Elijah, falls over them?"

"Miss Fitzgerald does not understand ghosts." Andrews told his companions as if he was lamenting Clara's scepticism, "The tripwires are to avoid fraud, Miss Fitzgerald, not to trip every soul who decides to go for a walk in the middle of the night."

"And the bells?" Clara asked.

"Ghosts have been known to ring them. In fact bells hold a fascination for the supernatural." Andrews puffed up his chest as he got onto his favourite subject, "I remember a case in Scotland, I was up in the Highlands at this old shooting lodge said to be haunted day and night by an old gamekeeper who had shot himself. It was the first time I had used bells on wires and it was quite remarkable how the ghost was attracted to them and rang them. In fact, you could track the progress of the ghost about the building by the bells he rang."

"I will be conducting a séance later." Bridget Harper interrupted in that oddly ethereal tone she had made quite her own, "You should attend."

"I don't do séances." Clara said firmly, "Last one I attended the medium ended up dead."

Bridget was unmoved. She gave her shoulders a slow shrug and then turned away.

"I want to use that room." She pointed to the library.

"We shall have it all arranged." Andrews assured her, "Now, if I might show you up the back stairs so you can get a feel for the place."

Clara turned to Oliver as the band of ghost hunters moved off.

"You don't believe this nonsense, do you?" She asked him.

"Not a lot of it, but it was odd about the camera. Here, let me show you something." Oliver fudged in his pocket and pulled out a photograph, "The plate was pretty badly smashed, but a few fragments remained and I wondered if I might be able to get an image off them. I fixed them into a fresh frame as best I could and then developed a photograph from them. This is what I got."

Oliver handed over a grainy image with a large jagged line cutting vertically down the centre. It showed the hallway in a brief moment between the flash going off and Elijah knocking over the camera, as such the image was slight blurred and twisted at an angle. An arm was just visible at the bottom of the image – apparently Elijah's as he tumbled backwards – but it was the strange form in the middle that caught the eye. The large line caused by the cracking of the plate had marred most of it, but just discernible was the outline of the back stairs door and, it seemed, a figure in a black cloak was hovering just before it. Clara examined the picture for several moments.

"Could it be a trick of the light?"

"Yes, possibly, but I can't see how. It looks like a figure to me."

"Elijah said he thought he saw someone."

"Yes."

Clara handed back the picture.

"Could be Jane." She said, "Then again, it could be our 'ghost' at long last."

"A real person, then?"

"Or an oddly cast shadow. Look, if the captain starts keeping watch with a shotgun in his hands, you'll stay out of the way, yes?"

"Not concerned about me, are you Clara?" Oliver grinned.

"I just would prefer everyone alive on Christmas day, that's all."

As she spoke Annie ran up behind her.

"Clara! I must speak with you immediately."

She almost made Clara jump.

"What's the matter?"

"I don't want anyone else to hear!"

Clara motioned to her bedroom and Oliver followed the two women as they went inside and closed the door. Annie was breathless as if she had been running around the house looking for Clara.

"I just heard something awful!" She declared, pacing back and forth across the room, "I was on the back stairs cleaning with Jane and I heard Mr William Henry Sampford talking about getting rid of his aunt!"

"Oh dear." Clara dropped onto the edge of the bed, "Are you sure?"

"Yes, I heard him talking about it to his wife. Something about him making several trips to London over the last few months and that he was going to take care of his aunt, but not in a nice way."

"All right Annie, keep calm. He can't do anything while we are in the house."

"Can't he?" Oliver interrupted, "Seems to me that would be the best time, when there were plenty of suspects on hand to shift the blame onto."

"Nothing is going to happen to Miss Sampford while I am here." Clara said firmly, "Annie, you best get back to the kitchen before you are missed and impress upon Jane that she must say nothing, especially to her mistress."

Annie nodded.

"More than ever I am certain this ghost nonsense is a blind, a means to distract us from what is really going on here." Clara said, "But it won't distract me. Let Andrews and his cronies bumble around in the dark after spectres I have a very living culprit to catch, and I intend to get them before they commit their crime."

"Well if I was a ghost." Oliver said with mock seriousness, "I would certainly be worried."

Clara put her tongue out at him.

Chapter Ten

Clara had refused to participate in séances after her unfortunate experience back in Brighton. She felt they were a dangerous game that brought the worst out in people. However, her distrust of Andrews and his colleagues meant that she at least felt she should observe what they were up to in the library. Besides, Miss Sampford had been asked to be present and she wanted Clara with her for moral support. Clara sat on a chair in the corner of the room watching as Captain Adams and Simon Jones set up a table in the middle of the room. They placed on it paper and a planchette board. Bridget Harper was meditating by the fireplace, a constipated look on her face that implied deep concentration. Clara was watching her most of all; she really didn't trust mediums.

"There has never been a ghost in this house before." Miss Sampford whispered to Clara.

"There isn't one now." Clara replied reassuringly.

Andrews checked that the curtains at the window were fully drawn, then he set to work lighting numerous candles that he had perched all about the room.

"Have you ever wondered why ghosts are so inordinately fond of the dark?" Clara mused, watching the ghost hunter in action, "I mean, as living beings we spend all our time finding ways to make the world brighter and to light up our homes. Why should our spirits be quite the opposite?"

"I don't know." Miss Sampford admitted, "I hadn't considered that before."

"It's just one of those things that doesn't make any sense to me." Clara shrugged, "But then ghosts don't make much sense to me at all."

Andrews finished with his candles and went over to Bridget. He touched her very lightly, but she still emerged from her trance with a start. For a moment she looked scared and confused, then she calmed herself and that air of detachment returned. She accepted the hand Andrews offered her and walked over to the table.

"Miss Sampford would you kindly join us?" Andrews pulled out a chair for his hostess and she reluctantly went over and took it, "I take it Miss Fitzgerald that you will remain purely as an observer."

"That is quite correct."

Bridget's pearly gaze drifted over Clara. She showed no sign of dislike or consternation over Clara's refusal to join them, she just watched the private detective in her unpleasant, distant fashion.

"Captain if you sit here. Mr Jones there. I will remain this side."

Andrews arranged the people around the table, soon all five were seated. Miss Sampford was almost opposite Bridget, while on her right sat Andrews and her left Jones and Adams.

"Miss Fitzgerald, if you would be so kind as to turn off the light?" Andrews said, with more than a glint of displeasure in Clara's direction.

She stood and turned off the light. The brightness of the artificially lit room faded to the dim flickering of candlelight.

"We should all place a finger on the planchette." Andrews continued.

"W... what?" Asked Miss Sampford.

"This wooden board on the table." Andrews explained, "It has a pencil in it so it can write."

"Oh." Miss Sampford reached out her hands, "Like this?"

"Just lightly, that's it. Now empty your mind of thoughts and Mrs Harper will conduct us safely through the process."

Bridget was by now breathing very deeply. Her eyes were shut and her head lolled forward. She rested just the very tips of her fingers on the planchette board and almost at once it began to move. From her seat Clara could not see the movement, but she could hear the faint rustle as the pencil ran over the paper. There was a 10 second spasm of activity and then the planchette fell silent.

"What did it write?" Simon Jones asked eagerly.

Carefully the planchette board was lifted and the paper removed. Andrews held it perilously close to a candle.

"Could it be meant to read 'help me'?" He postulated.

"Surely that is a 'D' rather than an 'H'." Challenged Captain Adams, "I think it is a name, Delphne, perhaps?"

"Daphne, maybe?" Simon Jones offered.

Clara sat very quietly in her corner finding the whole matter preposterous. She had begun that year at a séance and here she was ending it in the same way; she was not terribly amused. Andrews was now rambling that the message might be in Latin. Clara rested back in her chair and let her eyes shut. For a haunted library the room seemed very peaceful and she was very tired. She could almost drift off where she sat and she doubted she would miss anything significant.

"Supposing that first letter is an 'M'? 'Me lame'? Could it be an illiterate spirit?" Simon Jones suggested.

Clara wanted to say something but held her tongue. Overhead there was a thump of footsteps. William Henry Sampford and his wife heading for bed, she supposed. The thought of them sent a shiver down her spine. What was William planning to do to his aunt? If he intended for her to die of fright he was certainly managing a fair job. So far Miss Sampford seemed scared out of her mind and only her dogged stubbornness had prevented her from evacuating her home to somewhere less haunted.

"Perhaps we should ask the spirit for clarification?" Andrews had finally tired of the indecipherable script and placed a new sheet of paper under the planchette, "Let's ask a direct question. Is there a spirit in the room?"

As Andrews' voice tailed off the planchette began to move, making scratchy progress across the paper. After a moment it stopped and the board was lifted.

"I do believe that is a 'yes', what do you say captain?"

"Could be, could be."

"Are you the spirit haunting this house?" Andrews asked as he placed back the planchette.

Again there was the scratch of pencil on paper.

"Another 'yes', we are on to something!" Andrews hastily changed the paper for fresh, "Could you give us your name?"

The planchette danced.

"What does that say? Is that a 'V'? Violet maybe?" Andrews handed the paper to Simon Jones.

"Violet looks a good guess, that long stroke is most definitely an 'L'." Jones confirmed, "Do you know of any 'Violets', Miss Sampford?"

Miss Sampford was shaking a little, the movement of the tiny board beneath her fingers had spooked her and made her want to look over her shoulder. The thought of a spirit being in the room alongside them was enough to unnerve her for good, only Clara's silent presence made the whole experience bearable.

"There were a few in the suffragettes." Miss Sampford said, her throat as dry as dust, "None ever lived here as far as I am aware."

Clara made a careful note in the little book she carried. Bridget might not be in communication with actual spirits, but she had gotten her information from somewhere. Perhaps she knew something Clara didn't?

"Could someone go upstairs and tell them to quieten down?" Andrews said, his usual bad temper flaring, "I can hardly hear myself think."

The footsteps above had certainly gone on for some time, it seemed as though William Henry was pacing in his room.

"It is simply distracting, someone has to speak with him." Andrews' eyes flashed to Clara and she knew what was coming, "Miss Fitzgerald, if you wouldn't mind?"

Clara gave a small sigh and stood up.

"Will you mind me going Miss Sampford?"

"I will be fine dear. Just mind William's temper."

Clara lightly touched Miss Sampford's shoulder as she went past. She took the main stairs up to the third floor wondering how she would broach the subject of silence to William Henry. She doubted the volatile man would have much sympathy for the feelings of those involved in the séance. She was a tad surprised to find the hall lights on the third floor all off, but then perhaps William Henry had gone up with a candle. She could still hear him pacing as she turned on the lights.

William Henry's room was at the far end of the corridor. Clara could see a light coming from beneath the door. It reminded her how Annie had overheard the conversation in that room just a few hours earlier. She really needed to speak with William Henry when the opportunity emerged, but not tonight. Tonight she had her duty to Miss Sampford. She strode to the bedroom door and knocked.

"Mr Sampford?"

The pacing continued unabated, but she thought she heard someone mutter something gruffly.

"Mr Sampford, might I have a word?"

Still no one opened the door. Clara heard quite distinctly the words, 'go away'.

"Mr Sampford, would you mind not pacing so loudly? Mr Andrews has protested. He finds it distracting." Clara hated doing the ghost hunter's dirty work, "If it was up to me I would quite happily let you pace all day, but the silly man is playing with his planchette."

"Damn nuisance!" William Henry yelled at her.

Then there was a loud bang – like the shot from a pistol – and the light in the room went out. Clara took a step back from the door, at first stunned, then she regained her composure and ran to the door bursting it open. Fortunately it was not locked. She rushed into the centre of the room, not entirely sure what to expect, but half imagining there would be a body. She could see nothing in the darkness. She went to the wall and flicked the light switch. Nothing happened. The room was faintly illuminated by the light from the corridor. Clara could see enough as she tried to pick her way to the window without falling over anything and drew back the curtains. The moon was bright outside and let enough light into the room for her to see that there was no body lying on the floor or upon the bed.

On the mantelpiece was a candle. Clara lit it and took a better look at the room. On her right, as she faced the door was a fireplace, unlit, which caught her as odd since Flo had been told to light all the fires around 8 o'clock so the rooms would be warm for when people retired. Clara took a closer look and saw that the fire was still smouldering, but had been raked over and damped down. The matter was only getting more curious. On her left stood a tall, old-fashioned poster bed, the curtains of which were drawn back. Between the bed and the fire there was no space for a large man's body to fall and be hidden. That left only a single possibility; the bed was set in the middle of the room, there was a gap between it and the wall on the far side large enough for someone to fall down in and be hidden from view. It was not without considerable trepidation that Clara edged her way around the bed, her stomach tightening as she anticipated discovering the body of William Henry.

She peered down. The space on the far side of the bed was as empty as that on the other. Clara ducked down and stared at the bedside rug, the only thing on it was a pair of blue slippers. Clara stood sharply. What had just happened? She had heard William Henry, or at least someone in the room and she had heard what sounded like a shot. Yet clearly there was no one here. As rational and sceptical as Clara was, she had to admit the situation was rather disturbing, one might almost say spooky. But Clara was not about to accept that she had just witnessed a ghost; there had to be another solution.

Clara left the room still holding the candle. She closed the door firmly behind her, before pausing in the hall and considering her options. If William Henry was alive and well then she must not cause alarm – that would only heighten Miss Sampford's fears. On the other hand she was certain she had heard a shot. Deciding she had to treat the matter as if she had actually come across a body, she determined to secure the scene so no one might tamper with things while she went downstairs. She pulled a table away from the wall and wedged it in front of the back stairs doorway. It was a tight fit and no one would be getting through the door in a hurry. Then she turned and tested the handles of every other door in the corridor. They were all locked. Satisfied that it was now only possible to reach the room by coming up the main staircase (the attic rooms were only accessible by the back stairs), she headed back to the landing and made her way to the second floor. She paused to see who was about; there were muffled sounds coming from the library. Apparently they had heard nothing. Clara continued downstairs.

She headed straight to the drawing room, hoping to find all the remaining family there. If she did, of course, she would then have to reconsider what had just occurred upstairs, but no doubt there was a rational explanation for everything. She opened the door to the drawing room and found the majority of the house guests sitting in quiet activity. Hilda Sampford was busy on a piece of needlework, her husband was sound asleep on the sofa next to her, while Amelia Sampford was reading a glossy magazine and smoking. Clara took a mental note of who was missing.

"Where are the others?" She asked as lightly as she could.

"Went to play cards in the snug." Amelia lazily waved her cigarette at Clara.

Clara left the room as calmly as she could and went to the snug. She spotted Humphry heading in the same direction with a tray of sandwiches.

"Poor Mrs James, still at work in the kitchen?" Clara asked carefully, there were still far too many people unaccounted for.

"Mrs James will be there some time, there are quite a few pots and pans to clean." Humphry said with his usual noncommittal tone.

"At least she has Flo and Jane to help her."

"Indeed." Humphry nimbly opened the door with his elbow.

Having ascertained that all the servants were accounted for and had apparently been down in the kitchen for some time, Clara followed him. She had almost convinced herself that her imagination had been fooling her and William Henry would be sitting at the card table looking very hale and hearty. Instead she only saw Elijah, Oliver and Tommy.

"Where is William Henry?" She asked.

"Said he was going to fetch another decanter of Scotch and never came back." Elijah sighed, looking glumly at the incomplete card game, "I say, do you play Bridge?"

"How long ago did he leave?"

"Long enough that we could order sandwiches and have them made." Oliver motioned to the tray Humphry had just placed on a side table, "Want one?"

Tommy was naturally more alert to his sister's behaviour and he sensed something was wrong.

"What is it Clara?" He asked.

"We need to find him, at once." Clara said, no longer able to contain her urgency, "He is not in the drawing room, please Humphry could you check the other rooms?"

"Certainly." Humphry gave a polite bow and left.

"Clara, what has happened?" Tommy insisted.

"I'll tell you once I know for certain if William Henry is missing. Otherwise it doesn't matter."

The three men looked at each other, baffled. Oliver helped himself to a sandwich, there seemed no reason to waste good food until it was clear something was wrong.

After ten minutes Humphry returned.

"Mr William Henry Sampford is not in any of the rooms on this floor." He announced in such a grandiose tone that Clara wanted to slap him.

"All right, Oliver, Elijah, we need to check the second floor."

The two men followed her upstairs. The séance was still going on behind the library door.

"Check your rooms." Clara instructed.

"Whatever for Clara?" Oliver asked.

"Just in case, I have to be certain." Clara left the two men to look in their rooms while she checked hers. It was empty, so was the dressing room. That left Miss Sampford's and Mr Andrews' rooms. She took a deep breath and braced herself for the furore she was about to cause.

"I need to borrow Miss Sampford and Mr Andrews for a moment." She said as she opened the door.

Andrews glared at her.

"You are disturbing the atmosphere!"

Clara held her temper.

"It is important. If you don't wish to come yourself might I borrow your room key?"

"What is it Clara?" Miss Sampford asked anxiously.

Clara decided to adapt the truth.

"We may have an intruder, I just want you to check your rooms…"

"I have valuable equipment in mine!" Andrews leapt to his feet, almost sending the planchette flying. Miss Sampford was more sangfroid as she rose.

They went into the corridor and searched their rooms. Andrews was back in a moment to confirm everything was fine in his. Miss Sampford's room was also undisturbed. By now Elijah and Oliver were back.

"You best explain this Clara." Oliver said anxiously.

"I am concerned that William Henry appears to be missing." Clara said gingerly.

"But, we heard him upstairs?" Miss Sampford said.

"That wasn't him." Clara said, avoiding mention of the empty room, "We need to find him."

"He only left the room for a decanter of Scotch." Elijah glanced at everyone as though they could explain things to him.

"Oliver, would you perhaps accompany me upstairs?" Clara was inching to the staircase, but her hope to quietly sneak away with Oliver to investigate was thwarted by Andrews and Elijah following.

She could not shake them off as she headed upstairs, and they were still following as she returned to William Henry's room. Nervously, almost expecting a body to have suddenly appeared in the deserted room, she opened the door. There was nothing. Oliver flicked the light switch.

"Bulb's gone." He declared.

"I heard someone pacing and talking in this room and then something that sounded like a pistol shot. The light went out and I hurried in expecting to find someone lying dead." Clara explained.

"Sounds like you heard a ghost." Andrews declared rather joyfully.

"Even if I was inclined to agree with you – which I am not – that does not explain the disappearance of William Henry." Clara said stoutly, "This is his room. I swear I heard his voice and now he is gone."

Elijah stepped into the room and glanced around.

"So where is he?" He asked rather pointlessly.

"We need to search the house from top to bottom." Clara commanded, "Perhaps he slipped outdoors without telling anyone, then he will reappear and we will all feel jolly silly. But then again…"

"Don't you think you are over-reacting?" Andrews was leaning in the doorway with a patronizing smile on his face.

"I do hope so Mr Andrews. Now, if you please, you have several people handy, if you might institute a search as unobtrusively as possible. I don't wish to raise undue alarm."

Andrews gave a shrug.

"It will be very amusing when William Henry strolls in the front door and you have to admit to being spooked by a ghost." He grinned.

For once Clara hoped he was right.

Chapter Eleven

They gathered the guests and Humphry to arrange the
search. Tommy was delegated to conduct the ground
floor search, Captain Adams the first floor, Oliver the
second, Clara the attic, and Humphry the basement and
garden. The only people not involved in the search were
Amelia, Miss Sampford and Bridget Harper. Amelia had
gone into a fit of hysterics and was now lying prone in the
drawing room murmuring that her husband was
murdered; Miss Sampford, who was rather shaken, had
been commanded by Clara to watch over her; and Bridget
Harper, who seemed too dazed out of her mind to be any
help to anyone, had been left with them. Everyone else
was assigned a floor. Clara had Hilda Sampford, Jane and
Annie in her party. It had been unanimously agreed that
the servants' private bedrooms should only be searched
by women. Clara hardly imagined William Henry would
be up there, but then there was just no telling. She had
hardly imagined he would disappear.

They scattered and for the fifteen minutes there was
the sound of footsteps all over the house and doors
swinging open and closed. On the attic floor Clara
insisted they turn on all the lights and search the rooms
from nearest to farthest, that way preventing any escape,
if there was to be one. Surely William Henry would want

to be found? Aside from the bedroom jointly shared by Jane and Flo, and the bedrooms of Mrs James and Mr Humphry, the attic was unoccupied and the spare rooms were used for storage. Clara searched among broken chairs, forgotten cutlery and a wardrobe full of out-of-date ball gowns, but there was no sign of a person. Jane and Annie reported that the bedrooms were empty and every hiding place searched, while Hilda Sampford confirmed she had checked that all the windows were locked as well as the small hatch to the roof. No one had left the attic, not unless they were clever enough to bolt doors from the inside behind them. Clara was about to disband her search party and admit she may have been mistaken when there was a shout from below.

Clara hurried down to the third floor. Oliver was standing in the corridor with Simon Jones beside him, looking grim. Clara went towards him and he put a hand up to stop her.

"You said you heard a shot?" He asked, "Clara, it's not nice."

Clara shook her head.

"It never is."

She moved past Oliver and peered around the door to the bedroom next to the one belonging to William Henry and Amelia. Lying prone on the floor was Mr Sampford. There was not much left of his face, except bone and blood. Clara felt sick to her stomach and had to turn away.

"Shot in the face." Oliver said, his mouth twisted into a grimace.

There was more pounding on the stairs and Mr Andrews appeared with Captain Adams. Simon Jones turned to his approaching friends and gurgled,

"Shot." Before sinking into a dead faint.

Captain Adams ignored the prone ghost hunter and pushed towards the door, he stared into the room with typical military stoicism.

"The pistol is still there." He indicated to a small bureau at the back of the room, under which could just be seen the handle of a pistol, "Done at close range. I would suggest he put the gun in his mouth and blew out his brains."

"Whatever for?" Clara tried to swallow down her horror, "Was there any hint he was suicidal?"

Everyone looked blankly at her.

"The door was locked. We had to get the master key from Humphry." Oliver said.

Captain Adams entered the room and felt in the dead man's pockets.

"Here is the original key." He held up a brass key to show them.

"So he locked himself in an empty room and shot himself." Clara said, feeling so sick she hardly knew how she was managing to remain standing, "We have to call the police."

"Agreed. And someone has to break the news to Mrs Sampford." Captain Adams stood with a groan, "Sad state of affairs."

"I'll tell her." Clara sighed, "I suspect we may need to call a doctor too for the poor woman."

"And someone better move him." Oliver nodded to the unconscious Simon Jones.

The captain tutted loudly.

"What a disgrace."

Between him, Andrews and Oliver they managed to hump Simon Jones down the stairs and into Andrews' bedroom. Clara headed to the ground floor where she asked that Humphry call the police and then she informed Tommy of the discovery upstairs.

"Nasty business." Tommy said.

"It still doesn't make sense though. Why was the light on in William Henry's room and why did it then go out? I can understand that perhaps I mistook which room the footsteps were coming from. But why was he pacing around in the dark?"

"A man about to kill himself is hardly thinking rationally. Perhaps he kept the light off just so no one would disturb him."

"And the light in his bedroom? Why did it go out?"

Tommy shook his head.

"I can't answer that one without looking at the room and as I can't climb the stairs you are on your own for this one."

Clara left her brother in the hall awaiting the police, while she went to break the news to Amelia Sampford. She was in the drawing room lying on a sofa with Miss Sampford nearby. Bridget Harper was also present, staring rather distantly into the fire. Clara coughed politely as she entered the room and Miss Sampford sprang up.

"You have found him?" She asked.

"Oh lord!" Amelia groaned.

"We have found William Henry, yes. I'm afraid he is dead."

Amelia gave a shriek and buried her head in her hands. Miss Sampford stared at her for a moment, then seemed to conclude the woman was a lost cause and returned her attention to Clara.

"What has happened Clara?"

"We found William Henry in the room next to his. The door was locked and it appears he shot himself with a pistol."

"Oh no! Oh no!" Amelia cried, rocking back and forth on the sofa.

"This is very unexpected." Miss Sampford found herself having to reach for a chair and sit down, her legs had gone quite weak, "I… I can't imagine William doing such a thing. Amelia, do stop making that awful noise!"

Amelia had been keening softly to herself. Now she gave a shuddering sob and turned towards the back of the sofa and buried her head in the upholstery.

"The police have been called. I don't imagine they will spend much time over the matter." Clara found herself staring at Bridget Harper, who had not made a move since she had entered the room; the woman was either completely oblivious to their conversation, or utterly devoid of empathy.

"There was no hint..." Miss Sampford rubbed at her elbows, looking suddenly frail, "Amelia, had he said anything to you?"

Amelia snuffled into the sofa cushion.

"Amelia, dear, you really can't go to pieces like this." Miss Sampford said rather sternly, "It will do no good. William is dead and that is that."

"You horrid witch!" Amelia suddenly sat bolt upright and yelled at Miss Sampford, "You don't care at all, do you?"

"He was my brother's son." Miss Sampford said stoutly, "Of course I care about him! Perhaps more than he deserved. Don't call me a witch Amelia when I know full well how you spoke of me behind my back. You wished me dead."

"Nonsense!"

"You were overheard discussing my death, natural or not, with your husband!"

Clara grimaced to herself. Jane had clearly not been capable of refraining from repeating the conversation she had overheard to her mistress.

"I have never wished you dead!" Amelia had flushed bright red, it was difficult to say if this was from fury or embarrassment at being caught out, "Even if I did never understand why my husband must keep you in luxury while we struggled to pay our bills."

"You forget, the money that paid your bills was no more your husband's than it was mine, it was my father's money, the majority earned during his lifetime. I can't help that neither my brother nor your husband had a head for investments and finance. Don't try and lay claim to money that was never yours Amelia!"

Amelia snorted, her face screwed up into mean petulance.

"Why should I suffer for an old spinster?"

"And so we see your real feelings!" Miss Sampford was triumphant, "I hope you live long enough for people to grow weary and tired of you Amelia Sampford! Then perhaps you will appreciate how it is to feel you are too old to be of value to anyone and will regret your callousness!"

"It's hardly callous to want to keep a roof over my head!"

"At the expense of a roof over mine!"

"Ladies, enough." Clara stepped in, "This is not helping anyone. Amelia, before the police arrive and start treading on everyone's toes, might I please speak with you?"

"Whatever for? You are on her side!" Amelia pointed a sharp little finger at Miss Sampford.

"Right now I am on no one's side. I just want to try and understand what happened to your husband."

"How do you mean?" Amelia's voice caught in her throat.

"I just want to piece together the parts of this jigsaw. A man leaves a card game for a decanter of Scotch and winds up dead in a locked room. Yes, perhaps it is suicide, but until I have all the information on the matter I can't say for certain. Please may we talk, for your husband's sake?"

"If he didn't shoot himself, does that mean he was murdered?" Amelia asked stiffly.

"We can't rule out an accident." Clara answered, noncommittally.

"You all forget one thing." Bridget Harper's soft voice cut into the conversation and made them all turn sharply towards the fireplace where the medium sat apparently in a dream, "The ghost, the Berkeley Square ghost. Spirits are not to be taken lightly."

"Ghosts don't kill people." Amelia sneered.

Bridget's eyes connected with hers. Suddenly the medium seemed alive with energy and unbridled fury.

"Dismiss them at your peril Mrs Sampford. As your husband did."

"William Henry had no time for ghosts!" Amelia declared.

"Precisely. Precisely. And some spirits take such disrespect very unkindly." Bridget's gaze fell back on the fire and she seemed to have lost all interest in them.

Amelia pulled a face which demonstrated without words the dislike and disregard she had for the woman.

"Will you speak to me now, Mrs Sampford?" Clara asked.

"Very well, it's about time someone listened to my side of the story." Amelia gave a scornful look at Miss Sampford and stood, "We shall speak in private."

"Agreed. Miss Sampford, might I beg the use of your snug?"

~~*~~

Clara moved the forgotten tray of sandwiches to one side as she entered the room. Just the sight of them turned her already knotted stomach. She motioned Amelia to a chair. Mrs Sampford glanced at the many photographs dotted about the room. She pointed at one.

"My wedding day."

Clara picked up the picture and recognised a much younger William Henry and a smiling Amelia.

"I had such hopes. So many of them came to nothing." Amelia sat in a chair, all her bravado and spite suddenly gone, "Why would she keep a picture of us when she hates us so much?"

"I think you underestimate Miss Sampford." Clara settled herself in another chair, "I don't think she ever hated her nephew."

"You think we are wicked people?"

Clara said nothing.

"It's not wickedness, we are all just trying to survive." Amelia continued, "The estate eats money faster than it comes in. William takes so to heart his responsibilities to the family property. Talk of selling it would kill him."

Amelia suddenly realised what she had said and almost choked.

"Maybe it did kill him." She said, almost in a whisper.

"How bad are things, really?" Clara asked.

"Bad enough. The house is falling apart, we've sold off the best heirlooms just to pay bills. People say turn away the servants, well that's all very well, but some have been with the family years and are too old to find positions elsewhere. To turn them away would be to make them destitute. Now that would be wickedness. As it is I have dismissed all the maids and William maintains the grounds with help from a single gardener. We eat frugally, never invite guests and try our best to keep the house standing." Amelia gave a sobbing sigh, "It is such a constant battle. In the hall is the remains of a medieval roof, it is in desperate need of restoration. The local historic society keeps pestering us to do something about it before it rots away. Do you know how much that costs? William spends his days trying to work out how he can afford to do all the things that must be done. There is a Tudor stained glass window in the chapel, in desperate need of re-leading before it falls to pieces, and a Regency orangery made of cast iron in the style of a pagoda, said to be one of a kind and rusting to dust as we speak. It all needs saving, but there is just nothing left to save it with."

"Many would suggest selling part of the estate." Clara said tentatively.

"They are heartless people!" Amelia snapped, "I don't expect you to understand. The Sampford's have owned that estate since it was bestowed on them by Charles II for their support during the Restoration, that equates to the better part of 300 years! You don't just discard such history, it's... it's horrible. William Henry could not bear the idea of being the last Sampford. You have to appreciate that as much as he loved living at Sampford Hall, he also regarded himself as a custodian of it for future generations. Not that we..."

Amelia pulled a face and flopped back in her chair.

"No one understands." She declared.

"I am trying Mrs Sampford. If your husband considered himself a custodian, who did he envisage leaving the hall to next?"

"Edward Sampford. He is the next male heir. After him it will go to Elijah." Amelia spoke sadly, "It disappointed us both gravely that we never had children to pass on our legacy to."

"I'm sorry about that."

"Don't lie Miss Fitzgerald, you are on Miss Sampford's side and you couldn't care less about me or my feelings. You are one of these modern single women who choose a 'career' over a husband and look down on those of us who value married life. It's why she picked you, two peas in a pod."

"You do me a disservice." Clara said calmly, refusing to be offended as that was clearly what Amelia desired, "I would appreciate you not judging me from the very little you know of me. You will only get it wrong."

"I might say the same." Amelia folded her hands together, "You have been listening to that witch and her thoughts on me. Has she told you I am interested in nothing but money? No doubt she paints me as black as she can."

"Miss Sampford has said very little concerning you." Clara answered truthfully, "Besides, I always make a point of forming my opinion of someone, good or bad, from first-hand experience."

"You are really very dull." Amelia snorted, "No wonder you are still single. Men do not like dull women."

"Goad me as much as you please Mrs Sampford, it won't stop me attempting to help your late husband."

Amelia turned her head away, propping her elbow on the arm of the chair and cupping her chin in her hand.

"William was not suicidal." She said slowly.

"He did have a lot on his mind."

"So does everyone!" Amelia barked, "William did not take his own life! I know him, I know that would not be his style."

"What was his style?"

"Working through problems, finding solutions, not just… giving up!" Amelia snapped her head round to face Clara, "How is this helping?"

"When did you last see William?"

"Just after dinner. I went to read a magazine and someone suggested a game of cards. They needed a fourth hand for Bridge and no one knew how to play except William. He was roped into the business and they came here, to the snug."

"The other card players tell me William left the room a little while later for a decanter of Scotch?"

"William liked a drink in the evenings." Amelia smiled at the memory.

"But he never came into the drawing room for the decanter?"

"No!"

"Any reason he would go upstairs?"

"No."

"What about the pistol? Did he own one?"

"No!" Amelia suddenly burst into tears, "I can't stand it anymore! I don't want to answer any more silly questions! Leave me alone!"

She leapt from her chair and bolted out of the room. Clara let her go. She doubted there was more to be said. It seemed William Henry had reason enough to consider taking his life. Mounting pressures both emotional and financial could easily have tipped him over the edge. There was no reason to expect any other scenario, there was certainly little benefit to Amelia in his death, she would now be lumbered with the estate. Unless, of course, she planned on selling it. Clara suspected such a shrewd man as William Henry would have made that impossible in his will, perhaps tying up the estate in some sort of trust for Elijah to ultimately inherit, so the property remained in Sampford hands.

That seemed a lot of fuss for old bricks and mortar. Better to sell it to someone who could look after it, then cling to it and let it rot to nothing for the sake of familial pride. She got up from the chair and walked into the hallway. A police constable was stood at the front door and a detective was interviewing Humphry. Upstairs there would be more policemen studying the crime scene and preparing William Henry's body for removal. Then there would be statements taken and evidence collected, until everyone was satisfied William Henry had killed himself. Suddenly Clara felt very tired, but there was nothing else for it. She braced herself for a long night ahead and hoped the 'ghost' would have the decency to avoid haunting the house for the next few hours.

Chapter Twelve

Clara did not fall asleep until the early hours of the next morning, which happened to be Christmas Eve. Despite this she woke at 6am and determined to get up and to business before the rest of the household was awake. The bedroom was icy cold as she slipped out of bed; no maid had yet arrived to light the fire. She dressed as rapidly and quietly as she could, so as to avoid disturbing Annie – the poor girl had spent most of her night in the kitchen consoling Mrs James and the maids and persuading them, yet again, not to abandon the house as soon as dawn broke. William Henry's death had everyone shaken.

Clara pulled her curtains open a fraction, just enough to glimpse the world outside and to see that a light snow had fallen in the night. Clara was strangely pleased by this sight; snow showed footprints, should the ghost have been prowling around in the night there might just be some evidence. Not that anyone appeared to have witnessed anything supernatural during the commotion – perhaps even ghosts had a sense of decorum?

Clara collected her notebook and pen and headed upstairs as noiselessly as she could. Distantly the rumblings of the kitchen whirring into life could be heard. Mrs James would be trying to prepare a suitably festive breakfast and no doubt Humphry was laying out the dining room table. How many of the house guests would feel much like eating was another matter, but one couldn't break with tradition, could one?

Clara slipped past the room belonging to Edward and Hilda Sampford, only pausing a moment to listen to the faintest of snores. Their room was at the far end of the corridor, nearest the main stairs, and about as distant as it was possible to be from William Henry's room. Amelia Sampford had (naturally enough) refused to sleep in her own bedroom that night. Nor could she bear to reside on the same floor as the one on which her husband committed suicide. After much discussion she had switched rooms with Elijah and he had taken over one of the other guest rooms on the third floor.

Clara came to the room in which William Henry had met his end. It was an unused box room without a fireplace or bed. Perhaps at one time it had served the purpose of a dressing room for guests, now it was barren except for a large old rug across the centre of the floor. Clara stepped inside, turned on the electric light and looked around. There was not much to see; a forgotten print of a Hogarth cartoon hung on one wall, faded with time. On another wall was a sad watercolour of flowers in a vase, executed by an amateur hand and now damaged by damp. A small chest of drawers sat between two tall, narrow windows with thick drapes. Clara carefully closed the door behind her and went to the chest. She opened each drawer to assure herself they were empty. Clara now noticed the pale green striped wallpaper and the marks on the wall where other paintings had once hung. She could also clearly see the dark red stain, almost black, on the large rug.

William Henry had been standing with his back to the watercolour flowers when he died. He had been almost parallel with the doorway when found, but must have been standing further into the room, since he fell backwards without hitting the wall, which he surely would have done had he been level with the door when he was alive. Clara paced the room, working out where William had stood. She placed herself on the rug in the position he must had been and observed the room around her. In front was the Hogarth print, showing a scene of debauchery and drunkenness, to her right was a window. Clara imagined holding a pistol to her mouth. She found herself wondering what was the last thing in that room that William Henry had fixed his eyes on as he pulled the trigger.

Morbid thoughts. She turned around and looked at the blood stain on the floor. A lot of blood. She assumed it had been quick. So, William Henry had come into the room, locked the door behind him and shot himself. It was all very obvious and Clara could give no reason for the slight pang of doubt that assailed her as she considered it. No one else had been in the room. It was locked from the inside. Everything pointed at suicide.

Clara left the room and headed into William Henry's bedroom. It still troubled her about the light going out. She was just about convinced that she had mistaken the footsteps next door as coming from this room. But what was the explanation for the sudden blackout? William Henry could not have controlled it from the dressing room.

Clara lit a candle and pulled a chair over from the side of the bed and placed it under the light fixing in the centre of the room. Then she climbed on it and reached up for the bulb. She stopped just before her fingers connected with shattered fragments. The bulb was smashed, or perhaps it had popped? Ironic it had chosen the same instant William Henry had shot himself to explode. Clara didn't do ironic. She got back off the chair and stared at the light. A thought struck her, it was an old geometry puzzle she had once had to master at school, calculating the angle that a ball would fly at if kicked in a certain place. Clara slowly drew a mental line between the burst bulb and the wall that adjoined the unused box room. Angles were important, they could lead to such strange events.

She went to the wall and took a good look at the heavily patterned paper. It was not easy to make out anything in-between the swirls of dark blue and gold that twisted in gothic fashion all across the wall. After a moment of staring in vain she searched she fetched the candle. Holding it close to the wall, she searched the paper in the rough area that coincided with the position of the light fixing. Slowly working upwards, avoiding the confusion of the mad swirls and intricate patterns, the flicker of the candle illuminated an odd shadow. Clara stepped closer. The yellow light traced the edges of a hole in the wall. A very small bullet-sized hole. Clara had her answer. This was a stud wall, perhaps dividing up a once much larger room. When William Henry shot himself the bullet had nowhere to go but through his skull and into the wall. It slashed through the paper and, its speed rapidly decreasing, slammed into the light fixing, breaking the bulb.

So that was it. So simple and not a ghost in sight! Clara was pleased she had solved one mystery, but confusion still remained. Had William really taken his own life? There had been no note and Amelia seemed set against the idea, but then she wouldn't be the first wife who failed to understand her husband's innermost thoughts.

Clara wondered how long she had before the rest of the household woke up? She had an idea, but it went against the grain and seemed decidedly dishonourable. It would not be good for anyone else to catch her. Thing was, this might be the only chance Clara had to take a really good look around William Henry's room. It seemed rather deceitful and a bit sneaky, but if she didn't take the opportunity now she might never know the truth about last night. Amelia would have ample time to remove anything she deemed bad for the reputation of the family.

Her guilt assuaged, Clara set to work exploring the room. She confined herself to items that looked likely to belong to William Henry – of course Amelia's belongings might contain a clue or two but exploring the private possessions of the living somehow felt a lot more wrong than exploring those of the dead. She went through the side tables by the bed and a case that contained William's cufflinks and watch. She explored the chest of drawers, feeling in pockets for forgotten slips of paper and finding none. She went to the wardrobe and examined William's clothing, and finally turned her attention to his suitcase, still standing in the corner. It was not locked and she hoped to find papers inside. Instead she found a lot of bank notes, a quick count suggested something in the region of a thousand pounds, all just sitting in a case on the floor.

Clara closed the suitcase and stood up. Who carried that sort of money with them? Not allegedly hard-up gentlemen. But here it was. Did Amelia know about this? Clara suddenly felt a little giddy; there were only a handful of reasons she could think of that would make someone carry large sums of money around, and most were of the illegal variety. Blackmail sprung to mind. Annie had overheard Amelia say something about William Henry's regular trips to London. He had no business in the city and could hardly afford the trips for pure pleasure. What was so pressing to bring him to the capital? Blackmail was also a very strong motive for suicide. The pressure to find more and more money, the fear that the blackmailer will reveal what they know, it could all lead to such dreadful despair that their seemed only one way out of.

Then again, what if this wasn't William Henry's suitcase? What if he was the blackmailer and this was his pay-off? Clara decided she needed to let this information simmer for a while before she came to a conclusion. She needed a lot more evidence as well, but the money was a mystery.

Clara let herself out of the room without anyone seeing her. It was still early, but she did not doubt that Miss Sampford would be rising soon. She headed downstairs to the dining room and found a breakfast spread laid out that would have warmed the cockles of any country squire. Sausages, bacon, fried eggs, scrambled eggs, toast, black pudding, kippers, kedgeree. It was a feast that seemed far too jolly on a dark morning like this. Clara picked up a plate and took some scrambled eggs and toast. There were little ceramic pots of butter. She helped herself to one and sat down at the dining table facing the window. Outside the first workers were ambling down the road to begin yet another morning of labour. She saw a chimney sweep go past, followed by the milkman with his cart and large churns of milk. Just because it was Christmas Eve the city did not stop. She was beginning to think about having some more eggs and toast when Humphry appeared.

"I apologise madam, I was not aware anyone had come down as yet."

"I'm an early bird." Clara smiled.

"Would you care for some tea?" Humphry had a large teapot in his hands, "Freshly made, this is around the time the mistress comes down, so I always have the pot ready for her."

"Tea would be lovely." Clara said.

Humphry poured precise quantities of milk and tea into a small porcelain cup, then offered Clara the sugar bowl.

"No thank you." She turned it away, "I hope you managed to get some sleep after the commotion last night."

"I am well rested madam." Humphry said with his usual lack of emotion.

"Queer business. I wish I knew why the man had done it. This rather casts a pall over Miss Sampford's festive plans."

"I dare say we shall manage." Humphry took his stiff upper lip extremely seriously.

"She doesn't need this on top of the ghost nonsense. I wouldn't blame her for kicking that silly man Andrews out of the house." Clara was hoping to draw Humphry out, but it appeared she was failing for he gave no reply.

"Do you believe in ghosts Humphry?"

"They do not assist towards the smooth running of a household."

"I'll take that as a no."

"Indeed, madam."

Just then Miss Sampford appeared at the dining room door.

"My dear, you are up early."

"I couldn't sleep." Clara admitted, "Last night had me thinking hard."

"Me too." Miss Sampford took a seat. She looked rather shaken and pale, "Humphry, might you fetch me a plate of kedgeree?"

"Certainly madam." Humphry was in fact already in the process of placing the rice mixture onto a plate. As he placed the dish in front of Miss Sampford he presented a toast rack full of crisp white slices to Clara, "I thought you might appreciate a little more madam, on such a cold morning."

Clara was impressed at the man's intuition.

"Thank you Humphry."

"I still can't believe my nephew is gone from us." Miss Sampford plucked at her rice with a fork, "I suppose Amelia will wish to go home. She shouldn't be alone at a time like this though. I wish I knew what had driven him to it."

"Amelia seems to doubt he would even have contemplated suicide." Clara said cautiously.

"Wives often refuse to see what is right before their eyes when it comes to their husbands. Though I admit it baffles me also."

"William Henry had a lot of problems concerning the family estate, though?"

"Mostly of his own creation, but I suppose that makes little difference." Miss Sampford sighed, "And of course they never had children. I am not the sort of woman who berates the failures of others when it comes to producing offspring, but I know William Henry wanted an heir and Amelia is bitter that she never gave him one."

"Was there ever another…" Clara stopped herself from being indelicate, she fudged around with a piece of toast to give herself time to rephrase the question, "What of acquaintances? Friends who might have known he was depressed or anxious?"

"You may have noticed William Henry was not the sort for friends. What were you going to ask me before that?"

Clara pulled a face.

"Miss Fitzgerald, surely you are aware by now I am not easily shocked. Please, speak your mind."

Clara still toyed with her toast, then she looked directly at Miss Sampford.

"Is William Henry likely to have sought the attentions of a woman other than his wife?"

Miss Sampford gave a wry smile.

"Possibly. But he never told me about it."

"He was making frequent trips to London in recent months without specifying to his wife why." Clara refrained from mentioning the money in the suitcase.

"That is interesting. I didn't know, since he certainly didn't visit me on those occasions. I'm afraid probably the only person who can tell you more about what he got up to in London is William Henry himself."

"Yes, I suspect you are right."

After finishing her toast (of which she had consumed far too much and felt quite stuffed) Clara went to see her brother. Tommy was sitting in his wheelchair pulling a pair of gloves onto his hands.

"Ah, there you are old girl. Don't suppose I can bother you with a slight diversion?"

"What is it? I could do with escaping this drama for an hour or two."

"I wondered about going to see the Cenotaph in Whitehall?" Tommy pulled a newspaper cutting from his pocket, "It's not far from the tomb of the unknown warrior in Westminster Abbey. I would like to go pay my respects."

"That sounds like a jolly good idea to me. I don't expect much to take place here until tonight anyway, when those ghost hunters get going once more."

Clara went for her hat and coat, and before long they were weaving their way through London, having to walk most of the way as the omnibuses were quite a struggle with a wheelchair. It took them half an hour and the brisk pace soon had Clara rosy-cheeked and quite hot in her thick wool coat. The Christmas Eve rush was in full swing; the last minute shoppers were running madly from place to place trying to find the right gift. Clara saw more than one come close to a collision with a car as they dashed across the street. The shops were gaily lit up, with trees in their windows and quite a few boasting large ornate Father Christmases in their displays. The jolly fat man beamed out at the world, like some heathen god of Christmas.

In Whitehall a Salvation Army band was playing in their smart black coats, brass trumpets and tubas gleaming in the wintry air. Clara threw a coin in their collection box as she went past.

"Supposing William Henry was murdered." Tommy suddenly declared as they veered down another path.

"How?"

"I don't know. But the man was in a houseful of suspects. Plenty of people wished him ill."

The Cenotaph rose before them in crisp white stone, gently dusted with snow. A carved wreath hung on the side and beneath in large letters the words 'The Glorious

Dead' declared the monument's purpose. Clara came to a complete stop; the structure, which she had anticipated being much smaller, simply took her aback.

"The Glorious Dead." Tommy mouthed, "Sleep well my friends."

He reached into his pocket and drew out a slightly crushed sprig of holly.

"It was all I could find in the garden. Would you mind?" He held it up to Clara.

She took the sprig and went to the Cenotaph. She almost hesitated on the steps remembering that this stone monument was supposed to represent an empty tomb. So many had not come back, dead or alive. She rested the sprig of holly on the top step then retreated. Tommy stared at it a long time, tears glistening in his eyes. Clara reached out for his hand.

"Private Fitzgerald?" A tentative voice called out, "Do you remember me? Private Hawkins."

Private Hawkins was an older man, well-built but slightly stooped. He held out a thick hand for Tommy to shake.

"I remember you Hawkins." Tommy smiled up at the man, "How are you?"

"Not so bad, not so bad." Hawkins looked at Tommy's legs and bit his lip, "I didn't realise you were a Londoner."

"I'm not. Myself and my sister are down on a visit. Staying with some folks in Berkeley Square."

"Really?" Hawkins's face took on a curious twist, as though he was connecting two thoughts slowly, "Don't suppose you heard about that incident last night? That gentleman snuffing out his own life."

"News spreads so fast in a city." Tommy frowned, "That happened to occur in the house we are staying in."

"You don't say?" Hawkins was beginning to get excited, "Look, Fitzgerald, these days I earn my keep as a newspaper reporter and I have been wanting a scoop on that haunted house for months."

"I don't think Miss Sampford would appreciate the publicity." Tommy said coolly.

"Well, no, that's been the problem. But she can't keep a lid on this chap shooting his head off, can she? I've just been at the police station taking down the particulars. Coppers aren't going to follow it up, just a suicide to them. But I think there could be a story here, what with it happening in that house." Hawkins was almost gleeful as he thought of the possibilities, "Before you know it every journalist in Fleet Street is going to be camping on the doorstep, unless Miss Sampford protects herself."

At this point Clara intervened.

"What are you suggesting Mr Hawkins?"

"Every journalist wants a piece of that story. Haunted houses sell papers, especially haunted houses where someone dies in an unnatural manner. When I left the police station there were already a dozen other reporters heading in, all after the same information. I won't deny that your average journalist is a bit like a vulture, swooping in and tearing his own piece of meat from the carcass of a good story. That's how we operate. How we survive. Now the drama at No.50 is a prime story, something outside the realms of politics and the monarchy, perfect for the quiet spell newspapers have over Christmas. Every journalist wants to talk to Miss Sampford, their pens are all a twitch as we speak. The only way she can guard herself from all those story hungry vultures is to give an exclusive to one of them and give the others the boot."

"I imagine that exclusive would be to your paper?" Clara asked.

"Well, as it happens..." Hawkins shrugged his shoulders, "Look, I'll do a sensitive piece, even change names if she wants. Put her side across. But someone has to do something."

"Look here Hawkins, we are not here for your benefit." Tommy said hotly, before Clara put a restraining hand on his arm.

"Mr Hawkins, we cannot answer on Miss Sampford's behalf," She said calmly, "However, I do see your point. This story is too widespread for us to imagine the papers will simply ignore it. I am prepared to speak with Miss Sampford on your behalf, to suggest it might be in her best interest to tell her story to someone. But I want something in return."

Hawkins cocked his head, curious.

"What would you want?"

"Nothing that would set you out of your way, in fact, it will coincide with your interests. I want to know more about William Henry Sampford, for a start why he was paying frequent visits to London when he could ill afford them."

Hawkins' eyes lit up at this new nugget of information.

"That makes it even more interesting!"

"Do we have an agreement then?" Clara held out her hand to shake.

Hawkins took it.

"I'll see what I can dig up and I shall pop by around seven this evening to hear Miss Sampford's answer."

"That will be just fine." Clara said.

Hawkins doffed his hat to them and headed on his way. Clara and Tommy started back to Berkeley Square, Tommy rather moody.

"Why did you agree to that?" He grumbled.

"Because he is right. This story is going to have everyone camped on Miss Sampford's doorstep. At least an exclusive will bring her some peace and he can investigate places I can't. I need to know more about William Henry."

"Well, I don't trust him."

"I didn't say I did, but this is a situation where I need all the help I can get. Who better than a journalist to rake up every scrap of scandal about William Henry?"

"I hope you are right."

"There may be another advantage to this development. With all this publicity our ghost may think it desirable to stay away for a time."

"You still thing the ghost is a living person?"

"More so than ever." Clara wove them in and out of the crowds, "And I am starting to have a nasty feeling Miss Sampford is in a lot more danger than I first imagined."

Chapter Thirteen

The ghost hunters were at work when Clara and Tommy returned. Andrews was ignoring the suicide of William Henry as an inconvenience that need not interrupt his investigations. Bridget Harper was drifting around the third floor trying to pick up the vibes left behind by the deceased man. But aside from that, all attention was fixed on the second floor. Andrews was convinced he would obtain proof of a ghost that coming night and he had Oliver fixing up a remotely triggered camera. Clara simply tutted at them and headed for the drawing room.

There a glum Miss Sampford sat with Edward, Hilda and Elijah. Amelia was noticeable by her absence.

"Hello Clara, I wondered where you had gone." Miss Sampford looked up and gave a sad smile.

"I took Tommy to see the Cenotaph." Clara said.

"Ah, the place where that woman is supposed to have taken a photograph of all those ghostly soldiers on Remembrance Day."

Clara had not heard Andrews come in behind her. Now she turned and saw him.

"I am surprised you are carrying on with your investigations, Mr Andrews." She said coldly.

"Why would you be surprised?" Andrews asked innocently.

"It's in rather poor taste."

Andrews snorted.

"I am not investigating the man who died, so I hardly see your point."

"Please, do not fight." Miss Sampford had her hands clenched into fists and looked a picture of misery, "I can't take it today. My poor nephew is dead in my own house. I have given permission for Mr Andrews to carry on and so be it."

Andrews smirked at Clara.

"I am setting up a water experiment, would you care to see?"

"Not really." Clara said, "I have other things to do."

"As you wish." Andrews grinned at her again as he picked up an odd brass instrument from a side table and left the room.

"I know he annoys you Clara." Miss Sampford said as soon as the man was gone, "But having him and his strange experiments in the house keeps me from thinking about what happened last night."

"I understand." Clara placed a sympathetic hand on Miss Sampford's shoulder, "And I will continue my investigations as best I can."

~~*~~

Oliver had been tailing the ghost hunters all morning, in part to see if he could find any information useful to Clara, but also because he was extremely curious about the whole affair. Oliver was fascinated by the thought of ghosts, though he could not say for certain that he believed in their existence. The photograph he had taken that first night and developed from a badly cracked plate was extremely intriguing and he now wanted to know more. Just the thought of encountering the ghost of Berkeley Square sent a shiver of excitement down his spine. Oliver was sure Clara would scold him for such foolishness, but he couldn't help it. He was hooked.

Not that he understood what Andrews was on about with his buckets and shallow trays of water. Andrews had muttered something about ghosts being attracted to water and appeared to be creating a pathway of liquid obstacles for a spectre to follow – or rather for someone to fall over in the middle of the night and get completely drenched. Once again Andrews had sealed the staircase door, though nothing had broken his precautions the previous night. Possibly the ghost had been as disturbed as everyone else by the horrors of William Henry's demise. Oliver had to admit the thought of the man's obliterated face haunted him whenever he closed his eyes. He had seen some things during his time as a police photographer, but the scene upstairs would take some beating. No one, he concluded, should go to their maker looking like corned beef hash.

Bridget Harper was prowling about on the edge of Andrews' experiment with a volume of poetry in her hands. She appeared to have been reading the same page for some time. Oliver tried to observe her as Clara would; he saw a tall woman who liked to give the impression of being aloof and somewhat above everyone else. She was not precisely pretty, though her aura of mystery could be said to give her a certain charm to the right type of man. To be honest, she scared rather than enticed Oliver, she reminded him of a cat his aunt once owned. As a little boy he recalled how it used to perch on a table and glare at him, as if he was no more than some unspeakable worm it had just stumbled across. His aunt doted on that cat. Bridget Harper made him feel the same way; she even seemed to have the eyes of a cat. It didn't help that Bridget was apparently completely disinclined to speak to anyone today, particularly Oliver.

Facetious – that was a good word to describe her. Oliver felt quite satisfied with this description, perhaps he would make a detective after all. Simon Jones wandered over to him with a small bowl of water.

"Reminds me of the finger bowls the Chinese like to use." He said, showing the porcelain bowl to Oliver,

"Andrews' says you are going to try and photograph this ghost?"

"If I can." Oliver answered, "So far the ghost has been rather elusive."

"You find that quite often at the start of an investigation. It's the arrival of new people that does it. That's the reason Andrews likes to use the water experiment early on."

"Might I ask what it is intended to do?" Oliver tapped a copper jelly mould that had been upturned on a side table and half-filled with water. He wondered if Mrs James knew.

"Well, the theory is that ghosts can draw energy from moisture. It's why many hauntings occur near rivers or underground streams. Mr Lethbridge at Cambridge first proposed the idea. Andrews feels that by creating a corridor of water for the spirit to tap into, excuse the pun, he might lure it out. The plan is to make this place seem irresistible and also to increase the strength of any phenomena by giving the ghost plenty of energy to feed on."

"Sounds a little preposterous?" Oliver suggested, "I mean, it is just water."

"Ah, but is it? Turn water into steam and it can power an engine."

"That's a different principle."

"Really? Maybe ghosts are like steam engines and can somehow siphon off the water to power themselves? Look, I am man enough to admit there is a lot about this stuff I don't understand, but Andrews gets results." Jones beamed brightly, "We were at this old abbey back in the summer, lots of rumours of ghosts but nothing concrete. Andrews set up his experiments and within three nights we had stunning evidence that the place was positively heaving with foxes."

Jones laughed.

"Andrews is as happy to disprove ghosts as he is to prove them, that's my point and it is why I believe in his work."

"But how will he even know if the ghost is using the water?" Oliver asked.

"You'll get activity. Wait and see." Jones wandered off with his little bowl, looking for a place to put it down.

Oliver was about to disappear himself, and find out when lunch was being served, when he sensed someone behind him. He glanced over his shoulder and there was the haughty Bridget Harper glaring down on him.

"Your friend, the detective?"

Oliver blinked.

"Clara?"

"Her, tell her she needs to start believing in the unbelievable if she wants to solve this case."

"Clara doesn't really do the unbelievable."

"Just tell her she better start." Bridget Harper snapped shut her book of poetry with a thunk, "And tell her, William Henry did not choose to die."

Bridget moved away, much to Oliver's relief. He mused over her words. Clara was not going to like them one bit. Clara liked her facts hard and her ghosts purely fictitious.

~~*~~

With Miss Sampford in such a state of misery, it had been extremely difficult for Clara to broach the subject of giving an exclusive to Hawkins with her. Surprisingly the old lady was more amenable than Clara had expected.

"We suffragettes always recognised the power of the press." Miss Sampford explained with a tentative smile, "Yes, this Mr Hawkins is quite right that I won't be able to keep the press at bay now William Henry is dead. I believe I have already seen one loitering about, he has been standing under the trees in the Square and I quite think he is watching the house."

"I can't say it is ideal having the press involved, but this Hawkins fellow seems a necessary evil."

"I am under no illusions concerning the press." Miss Sampford shrugged, "They will print what pleases them. I suppose I ought to warn Amelia. She is talking about returning home this afternoon."

"I would prefer she stay here."

"So would I, but I expect our respective reasons for that preference are very different."

Clara left Miss Sampford in the drawing room and went to the dining room window to peep out into the Square. As Miss Sampford had said, there was a man lingering under a tree. He was reading a newspaper, but on a cold Christmas Eve it seemed a very preposterous activity. Clara couldn't see his face below the brim of his pulled down hat, but she suspected he was a member of the press come to get a scoop on the house. Well, he was to be disappointed.

Clara left the window and returned to the library. She turned her attention to the bookshelves, wondering if there might be any insightful volume to be found there. Perhaps one on the history of the house?

The library door handle turned lightly and Clara looked up. The library door swung open a little. Clara waited for someone to appear, but nothing more happened. She took a pace back and tried to see around the door.

"Hello?"

There was no answer. Clara went to the door and pulled it open. The corridor outside was empty; Andrews and his team had gone for lunch leaving the water experiment to its own devices. Clara glanced left then right. No sign of anyone. She took a step into the hallway and her foot squelched on something. Looking down she saw a small puddle of water on the floor.

"Damn Andrews!"

She went back into the library and shut the door. That was when she heard the footsteps scuttling towards the staircase.

Chapter Fourteen

"Let's start at the beginning." Hawkins flicked over a page in his notebook, "Tell me about William Henry."

It was half past seven in the evening and Hawkins had arrived late for his appointment. Clara was sitting in a chair by the fire feeling a little chilled and wondering if she was getting Tommy's cold. Miss Sampford was on the sofa opposite the journalist giving her rendition of the incidents of the night before. Everyone else was in the dining room eating dinner.

"Do you believe in ghosts, Miss Sampford?" Hawkins asked, his pencil flicking across the notepad in fast shorthand.

Clara rubbed her forehead with her fingers as Miss Sampford once more recounted her experiences in the house. Hawkins would want to interview Elijah next, then the troublesome Andrews. Before long he would have enough information for a series, let alone one article. And in a few hours it would be Christmas day. That seemed slightly unreal to Clara; how was anyone supposed to think about Christmas with all this going on? Amelia Sampford had somehow been persuaded to stay on at the house, but her misery was palpable and cast a shadow over proceedings. Everyone else was obviously shaken and no one wanted to talk about William Henry, which made conversation with Amelia tricky. Even Clara found herself hedging around safe topics and speaking the most inane rubbish to avoid upsetting her further.

"I cannot agree that my nephew's death was caused by this ghost." Miss Sampford was saying hotly.

Clara glanced up.

"The evidence is compelling, however." Hawkins was flicking back through his notebook, "There have been two other suicides and at least one suspicious death in this house over the last 200 years."

"Such things occur without any need for paranormal influence." Miss Sampford replied stoutly.

"Might I ask," Clara spoke up, "What the other cases were? I don't imply they were caused by the ghost, but they may provide a reason for the haunting."

She did not add that she still anticipated the person behind the haunting to be very much a living, breathing human being.

"Let's see," Hawkins went through his notes, "Right, 1893, the house was in the possession of a man called Mr Brooks, a bachelor who kept himself to himself according to the neighbours. One night he came over strange and threw himself from a window in the attic. He impaled himself on some railings in the fall and died soon after. Not a pleasant spectacle."

"Did he leave a note?"

"No, but his housekeeper said he had been morose for some time."

"What about the second suicide?" Clara persisted.

"1835, Mr and Mrs Penn were then living in the house for the season. Mr Penn was a plantation owner who had not made himself very popular with the abolition of slavery movement. He was outspoken and rather intolerant, from what I have read. Well, in the year I mentioned he had a cousin to stay and there was some sort of argument between the two. Mrs Penn could not state precisely what. But the cousin slit his throat with a razor the next morning and Mr Penn is said to have gone mad with remorse and ended up in an asylum."

"And the murder?"

"1788. House belonged to a minister called Benfold. Benfold had a wife and a mistress, the latter not being very secret. No one can say quite what happened, but one day there was a dreadful commotion in the house and the neighbours rushed in to find the mistress and Mrs Benfold both lying in a pool of blood in one of the rooms on the second floor. Benfold was apprehended trying to run through the garden with a bloody bayonet in his hand. He refused to say what had occurred but he was tried for murder and executed. Miraculously the wife survived, but the mistress was done for. Quite a few people place the blame for the haunting at the mistresses' feet, so to speak."

Clara nodded, that was similar to the story Flo had told Annie.

"This bears no relation to the matter of my nephew." Miss Sampford shook her head, "Now, you have your story, might I go eat my dinner?"

"Certainly." Hawkins grinned, "Sorry to have disturbed you."

Miss Sampford gave a small huff and left the room. Clara waited until she was gone.

"Your turn, Mr Hawkins."

Hawkins gave her that same cheesy smile.

"You want to know what I found out about William Henry?"

"Precisely."

"Seems the old boy wasn't quite what you would expect. He was a West End lad, if you know what that means."

Clara narrowed her eyes.

"I'm sorry, I don't."

"The sort who prefers the back row of theatres? Clearly this is new to the world of Brighton. Let's just say he had a lot in common with the unmentionable Oscar Wilde."

"Ah." Clara understood, "We are not so naïve in Brighton Mr Hawkins, but your terminology eluded me. William Henry was not a man who chased women behind his wife's back then?"

"Hardly. But he certainly chased men."

Clara nodded, things started to make sense.

"Anyone in particular?"

"Haven't come across a specific name as such, but his regular trips to London put him in all the right places for meeting the right fellows. I suspect he was after a casual fling, nothing serious."

"A dangerous game for any man, but especially one who so values his reputation." Clara said, "He would have been a ripe candidate for blackmail."

"Do you think that is what caused his suicide?"

"I couldn't say."

"Don't get cagey now Miss Fitzgerald." Hawkins winked at her, "Not as if my editor will let me print any such speculations in the paper anyway. Know how much trouble I could get in for such talk, no matter how true it is?"

"Quite. I don't suppose you have any names of folks I might call upon to tell me more?"

"They don't exactly give their names." Hawkins winked again.

"Hawkins, I need more. There is something very wrong in this household, I fear for Miss Sampford's life."

Hawkins was genuinely surprised.

"That dear old lady?"

"Yes. The problem is, out of the two suspects I had in mind for being behind this, one has a reasonable alibi and the other is dead. Yet we still have a ghost that seems a little too 'flesh and blood' for my liking."

Hawkins mused on this a moment.

"What do you want to know?"

"Two things, first I want to know for certain that William Henry's only reason for coming to London was to find companionship and nothing else. Second, see what you can root out about Miss Sampford's past. As awful as that sounds, I feel the clue to this mystery lies in our hostess and none other. She was a suffragette and quite political in her day, perhaps she made enemies?"

"Not much then." Hawkins snorted in amusement.

"If I was on my home turf I would be doing this myself, as it is I must rely on someone who knows this city inside and out."

"I appreciate your confidence, Miss Fitzgerald."

"Well, we shall see if it is well-placed. I think it is time I got to my dinner Mr Hawkins, and no doubt you have an exclusive to pen."

"I do indeed, and I need to get back to the wife, promised to take her to Midnight Mass."

"That sounds very pleasant." Clara escorted him to the front door, feeling no need to summon Humphry from his duties in the dining room.

Hawkins doffed his hat at her and strolled down the front steps whistling. Clara paused long enough at the front door to note that the man under the tree was still there and looking mighty cold. She closed the door and headed down to the kitchen.

"Mrs James, might I beg a few slices of that lovely beef you served for lunch in a sandwich and a hot cup of tea?"

Mrs James glanced up from a mulberry jelly she was carefully decorating with mint sprigs.

"Certainly madam." She disappeared into the pantry and returned after a few moments with a plate of cold beef and a large loaf of bread. As she cut and buttered the bread Clara kept talking.

"Where are all the house keys kept Mrs James?"

"Well the room keys are usually in the doors of the rooms, the front and back door keys are on hooks in Humphry's room and he also keeps a master key on him at all times."

Clara took note of this, it would have been easy for William Henry to remove the key from the unused bedroom door and lock himself inside with no one knowing.

"Please remind Jane not to come down the back stairs tonight. Mr Andrews has set up some ghastly water experiment. I fear we shall all be drowned by morning."

Mrs James smiled at the joke as she handed over a thick sandwich the size of a doorstep and a cup and saucer of hot tea.

"Will that be all Madam?"

"For the moment, now might I use the back door?"

Mrs James nodded and watched curiously as Clara carried out her refreshment into the snowy garden.

Clara had discovered the narrow alley leading from the back of No.50 to the main Square when she was on a hunt for footprints in the freshly laid snow earlier that day. Needless to say she had found none that could not be accounted for, which was deeply frustrating. But then the ghost had not appeared last night, so perhaps no one had been in the garden to make unaccountable footprints? Clara wondered how the ghost had caught wind of the drama at the Square. Yes news spread fast, but the perpetrator would likely have already been on their way to begin the haunting when the story broke. Unless they saw the police, of course.

She stepped carefully up a few steps and into the dim light of a streetlamp. Clara's breath formed foggy clouds in the cold night air. She strode across the road and straight towards the figure beneath the tree. The watcher was so wrapped in his coat, hat and scarf and so focused on the house, that he failed to notice Clara until she was right on top of him, and then he jumped in surprise.

"You looked cold." Clara held out the beef sandwich and tea, "Clara Fitzgerald, by the way, staying with Miss Sampford."

The man eyed the food suspiciously.

"It isn't poisoned." Clara said.

Cautiously, as if it might be booby-trapped, he took up the hefty sandwich and pulled down his scarf to bite into it. Clara glimpsed a fluffy moustache and a broken tooth as he devoured the offering.

"Thanks miss." He mumbled through breadcrumbs.

"Don't tell me you have stood here all day without food?" Clara held out the cup of tea, "That is really foolish in this weather."

The lurker looked abashed.

"I was told to stand here and watch. I didn't like to leave and get something to eat."

"Drink your tea." Clara pushed the cup into his hands, "Who told you to stand here anyway?"

"Can't say miss." The man's head seemed to sink into his scarf.

"Well, if you are newspaperman your editor is going to be very disappointed, because the gentleman who just left has been given an exclusive on the story."

"I don't work for the newspapers, miss." He took the tea and slurped at it.

"Then who has had you standing here all day? Really, it is quite ridiculous. We have been watching you from the window, so it is hardly a secret you are here."

"Really?" The man looked forlorn, "I'm no good at this lark. It isn't what I do normally."

"So what is your usual job?"

"I fit and repair floors. Got a loose floorboard, I'm your man, want some carpet laid, not a problem."

"But you aren't working today?"

"Nah, got today off. You see these last few weeks I've been working in No.49 sorting out the floors. Lot of dry rot in that building, I had to replace a whole chunk of the second floor. It was in a dreadful state, especially where some fool had placed a bathtub and let it overflow on a regular basis. Must have been every night for years. Floor contained more water than the sea!"

"Dreadful." Clara nodded sympathetically, "So you work for Mr Mollinson?"

The man's face fell.

"You won't tell him you saw me, will you?"

"Does he know you are here?" Clara asked, already guessing the answer.

The man gave a long sigh, realising the game was up.

"Mr Mollinson asked me to keep a watch on the house and Miss Sampford. Said he thought there was trouble brewing."

"What sort of trouble?"

"He said he thought Miss Sampford was making up all this ghost business to ruin his hotel venture, out of spite because of the pressure he had been putting on her. Said no one wants to stay in a hotel next to a haunted house, 'specially where someone has died."

"He heard about that then?"

"Yes, saw it in the early edition of The Times. He said I needed to watch what was going on and he would pay me double my normal rate if I did so."

"Well now, a fine spot of bother your Mr Mollinson has put you to." Clara patted him on the shoulder, "Go back to your employer and tell him that on my word of honour there is nothing going on here deliberately designed to harm him. There is trouble at No. 50 and I am here to attempt to stop things getting worse. Any assistance would be appreciated, but otherwise I wish him a very merry Christmas."

The watcher shuffled his feet and started to move away.

"Thanks for the food and drink, miss, and for being so understanding."

Clara shrugged.

"Tell Mr Mollinson if he wants to know anything more all he has to do is ask."

The carpet-fitter gave a little nod then scampered off, no doubt looking forward to warming himself before a good fire and airing the chill out of his bones. Clara headed back inside, satisfied that at least one small mystery was solved.

Chapter Fifteen

Clara lay in bed thinking about the slight sting at the back of her throat and the shivers running up and down her spine. She had drunk camomile and honey tea before bed, hoping to quash the illness that was threatening before it began. The last thing she needed was a full-blown cold in the middle of a case. She pulled the bed covers right up to her chin and tried to get warm. The house was silent; everyone was abed, except for Andrews' team of ghost hunters who were taking turns to watch for the ghost in the corridor outside. Clara had heard the hourly change over a few moments ago, Simon Jones replacing Captain Adams and his big shotgun.

Somewhere outside a clock bell rang the hour. It was 1am on Christmas morning. Very soon small children everywhere would be bouncing out of bed and insisting on opening presents. The butcher would open his shop to sell his last few geese and turkeys, the baker would pull up his shutters and offer hot bread to early morning shoppers, the religious would head through the cold to church and the newspaper boys would hawk the papers as they did every day of the week. Finally, just before dinner, the world would go quiet. The shops would shut, the stragglers would go home and for a few hours Christmas would be enjoyed (or endured) by almost everyone who was able to.

Clara tried to will herself to sleep. It was almost impossible. She was considering getting up and finding a book to read when she heard the soft sound of a bell beginning to ring before being abruptly silenced. Clara held her breath. Andrews had rigged his usual traps, the bell being just one of them, but no ghost would know to reach out and stop the bell from ringing, would they? On the other hand, a person, a living intruder, just might.

Clara strained her ears for any sound and there it was, very soft and careful footsteps coming from her left, from the direction of the back stairs. To her right she heard movement; Simon Jones rising from his chair. He had heard it too. Clara slipped her feet out of bed and reached out to try and find her dressing gown. Even as she did so she heard the sound of a bowl wobbling on a table, as if someone had bumped into it. Simon Jones sprang forward, she heard his feet moving, and suddenly another set of feet running. Simon Jones was in pursuit of something.

Clara's hand felt around frantically for the dressing gown, where was the damn thing? She heard a clatter, a splash and then the crash of porcelain as one of Andrews' water containers took a tumble. Clara gave up on the dressing gown and dashed for the door. Pulling it open she was just in time to see Jones flying through the door to the back stairs. Captain Adams, Oliver and Elijah were all coming out of their respective bedrooms.

"They went that way!" Clara announced turning to her left as she spoke.

She was about to dash after Jones, and was halfway down the hall, when Oliver suddenly grabbed her around the waist and halted her.

"Not over that!" He pointed to the floor.

In the glimmer of moonlight from his room could be seen shards of broken pottery dotting the floor. Had Clara carried on she would have cut her bare feet to shreds.

Adams came pounding down the hall after her.

"Someone clear up that mess." He ordered, his slippers flapping as he ran past, "Come on now!"

He was just about to leap over the debris and follow Jones when there was a sudden shout and then a cry, following by a series of thuds and crashes emanating from the back stairs. Clara went stock-still, she could feel her heart pounding in her chest. It didn't take a detective to know what had caused those noises.

"Jones?" Captain Adams went towards the door more cautiously now.

"He fell right to the bottom." Clara said very quietly, so only Oliver overheard.

"Jones?" Adams opened the door to the back stairs and peered into the darkness.

"What's going on?" Miss Sampford appeared at her bedroom door looking ashen, "What has happened."

"A bowl was broken." Elijah said as lightly as he could manage, stepping towards his aunt and shuffling her back into her room, "And Mr Jones has tripped on the stairs in the dark. It will be all sorted in a moment."

"Oliver, we have to go downstairs." Clara pulled away from the photographer and went to grab her slippers as Captain Adams hovered at the door of the back stairs, apparently unwilling to go down.

Clara and Oliver made their way to the basement area, where the back stairs emerged into a corridor next to the kitchen. There was a door at the bottom. Clara stood before it.

"I can do this." Oliver said.

Clara smiled at him wanly.

"I'm not scared of the dead." She said softly, then she lifted the latch on the door and pulled it open.

Simon Jones tumbled half out. His head flopped at Clara's feet, while his legs still lay on the stairs as he had fallen. Clara managed not to gasp, though she hopped back as the body slumped towards her. Falling three flights of stairs is never a good idea; it had certainly done

Jones no favours. Clara bent down and looked for signs of life.

"I'm pretty certain he is dead." She whispered to Oliver.

Oliver grimaced.

"He slipped, and all those narrow steep stairs are lethal." He shook his head, "Tragic."

Clara stood and stared up the staircase.

"He was chasing someone."

"The ghost?" Oliver glanced at the stairs too, "I heard nothing."

"That's because they silenced the bell." Clara was starting to feel very angry, "And they were treading very, very carefully, except they did not know about the water bowls. And when Jones spotted them they ran. Does that sound like the behaviour of a ghost?"

Oliver had no answer.

"Simon Jones was running upstairs, how often have you tripped running upstairs Oliver?"

Oliver shrugged.

"More times than I care to remember."

"And what happens?"

He gave her a curious look.

"You fall on your face, it hurts."

"I know, I've done it. You might slip a few steps, but not the whole way because you grab out with your arms. But you know, the one time I did fall properly down the stairs was when I was coming down, not going up."

"What are you saying Clara?"

"Simon Jones was running upstairs, if he tripped it's unlikely he would have fallen like this. No, he was either already heading back down when he stumbled, or…"

"Or?"

"Or he was pushed. Which makes our ghost a killer."

Oliver grimaced.

"Don't say that Clara."

"Why not when it is true? He was chasing someone, well, where is that person?"

Oliver peered at the stairs again.

"I think we ought to call an ambulance."

"All right." Clara said, "And in the meantime it would be best to call this a horrid accident and not speculate to anyone about murder."

"Agreed." Oliver pulled a face, "I've gone off this ghost hunting business."

"Oh, I don't know," Clara frowned at the body of Simon Jones, "I'm just warming up to it."

Chapter Sixteen

It had been another very disturbed night and Christmas morning arrived with a subdued air in the Sampford household. Somehow Mrs James had managed to whip up a Christmas breakfast that exuded the festive cheer no one else could muster. She was just about holding herself and the two maids together; the news of Simon Jones accident had not gone down well. It was fairly certain Jane would be leaving the following day, though Flo had promised to soldier on. Clara didn't want anyone to leave while the mystery of this murderous spirit remained unsolved. She was beginning to doubt everyone in the household, no matter how innocent they seemed.

After a stout breakfast that really should have seen them fit for anything, Miss Sampford and her brother and sister-in-law announced they were going to church and would return in a little while. Clara felt it was a good idea to get Miss Sampford out of the house for a time, she needed the fresh air. Simon Jones' death had shaken her to the core. She hardly said a word as she put on her hat and left with Edward and Hilda. Clara hoped she might have some answers by the time they returned.

As soon as they were gone, she headed upstairs, right to the top. She wasn't sure which floor Simon Jones had fallen from, but it had to be either the third or the attic, and somehow the third floor seemed to be drawing all her attention. She examined the landing in the attic first, just in case. There were no overt signs of a struggle, but then she hadn't really expected any. She came to the third floor and found Mr Andrews examining the door to the back stairs. He paused when he heard her footsteps and acknowledged her with a nod.

"Nasty business." He said quietly.

"I'm very sorry about Mr Jones." Clara replied.

"So am I. In all my years doing this I've never had someone die before."

"Had Jones been doing this long?"

"Oh, about five years." Andrews shrugged his shoulders, "I met him at a dinner in Oxford. I was guest speaker for a literary society Jones belonged to. He had read my book Forty Years as a Ghost Hunter. After a little discussion I agreed to involve him in one of my next cases. He proved very adept at tracking ghosts and very reliable. He was with me during the Wiggleford Forest expedition, when we were chased by something unspeakably horrid."

"He knew how to deal with ghosts then?"

"I should say so! Not that they precisely need dealing with. They are ethereal entities, spectral memories, nothing substantial. Most of the time we just prove they exist for the benefit of the frightened household, or for that matter, we prove they don't."

"And your thoughts on last night?"

Andrews gave her a sly look.

"Is this an interrogation Miss Fitzgerald?"

"Jones is dead, William Henry is dead, I don't particularly want the police around tonight too. So, yes, I have questions that need answering, but I am honestly interested on your thoughts about last night. Do you think he simply tripped and fell?"

"It's a dark staircase." Andrews said.

"True, and Simon Jones may have reached the top, found nothing, turned around to come down and fallen."

"But you are not convinced?"

Clara pulled a face.

"Just something about the way Jones fell, I don't think he was coming down the staircase, I think he was running up, maybe on the very last step. I think he fell with his back to the stairs."

"You mean he was pushed." Andrews cocked his head reflectively.

"I don't like coincidences." Clara continued, "The death of William Henry, apparently an unforeseen suicide, and now the seemingly accidental death of Jones troubles me. Two deaths in two nights strikes me as a pattern of sorts."

"Your standard ghost isn't much of a killer." Andrews mused, "Unless you want to look upon people who have been scared to death as murder. No, ghosts don't deliberately kill."

"Then at last we are agreeing on something, You see what this means?"

"Yes Miss Fitzgerald!" Andrews suddenly snapped his fingers, "It's perfectly clear now. It couldn't be a ghost!"

Clara felt like cheering, but restrained herself.

"Precisely, there has never been a ghost at Berkeley Square." She smiled.

"No, indeed! I have been looking at this all the wrong way." Andrews looked surprisingly jovial for someone who had just been proved wrong.

Clara started to feel uncomfortable.

"If Jones did not encounter a ghost last night..." She began, but Andrew interrupted.

"I should have considered this sooner, I once saw it happen in Ireland."

"I suspect Jones met a person last night," Clara quickly finished, "A living one."

"A person!" Andrews stared at her in astonishment, "Yet again you prove how naïve you are young lady. No person was on that landing!"

Clara folded her arms across her chest. The phrase 'young lady' had not gone down well.

"Honestly, it is fortunate for Miss Sampford I am here." Andrews chuckled to himself in his infuriatingly patronising manner, "A person? That was no person! The creature on the landing last night must have been an Elemental."

Andrews opened the door from the back stairs and stepped into the third floor corridor.

"An Elemental?" Clara called after him, curious despite herself.

"That would explain the attraction to water." Andrews was muttering to himself, "And the sudden appearance after years of no disturbances."

"Mr Andrews, you do appear to be babbling."

"Spare me your sarcasm Miss Fitzgerald. Jones was killed by an Elemental, a being of evil that was never alive, has never existed so to speak. Some refer to them as the spirits that dwell in nature. When disturbed they rise and take form and can often be particularly malevolent. Yes, that explains why Bridget struggled to fix on a voice during the séance, there was no spirit to communicate with! I'll need to change my equipment at once!"

Clara left Andrews to his enthusiastic ramblings, tutting to herself as she went back down the stairs. How anyone could believe in such nonsense was beyond her. Clara's next stop was the drawing room where she found Elijah sitting smoking before the fire. It was about time she had a good chat with the people relevant to this case, and Elijah happened to be one of them. She asked him to join her in the 'snug' and shortly afterwards they were tucked away in Miss Sampford's private room, overlooked by various family members peering from their photographs.

"How can I help, Miss Fitzgerald?" Elijah asked as soon as they were settled, he looked quite jaded behind his friendly smile.

"I'm trying to get my head around this business of the ghost." Clara began, "I hoped you might be able to help me. Perhaps we could begin by discussing your aunt?"

"My aunt?" Elijah looked blank, "What about her?"

"Do you like her?"

"Of course! What a silly question. She is a dear, old lady. Very sweet."

"And you like living here?"

Elijah lightly smiled and leaned forward in his chair.

"I understand what you are implying; nephews do bump off their aunts. However, I have no desire to do so. For a start it would leave me without a comfortable abode in London, I would have to rent a place and find servants which I would find most loathsome. Auntie has left me some money, I know that much, but that is really inconsequential since mother sees fit to supply me with a healthy allowance, most of which is accruing nicely in my bank account. I have no major debts and no need of auntie's money."

"You get on well with your aunt then?"

"Miss Fitzgerald, if I didn't, would I be spending Christmas here rather than with my mother?" Elijah sat back in his chair with a sigh, "I don't get on so well with mater, I don't really live up to her expectations. It's not that I don't try, I try extremely hard, but somehow I can't manage the top scores in exams and I seem to always annoy her. I would much rather be here. Auntie doesn't pester me about my results, she lets me come and go as I please. I feel she understands what it is like to be a disappointment to your parents."

Clara nodded sympathetically.

"What about your cousin, William Henry?"

Elijah shook his head.

"We hardly spoke, he was a great deal older than me. My late father was William Sampford's (William Henry's father's) younger brother by a number of years and married late in life."

"You must have had some opinion on him?"

"I mostly tried not to think about him. He was not exactly pleasant, and that awful wife of his, Amelia. I really wish my aunt would let her go home. I hear her sobbing and talking to herself in her bedroom during the night. It is most horrible, she sounds mad."

"Had you any suspicions William Henry was suicidal?"

"None." Elijah stuck out his bottom lip, "He didn't seem the sort, but I suppose you just don't know. We had this fellow at university during my first year who killed himself, drunk a mixture of carbolic and prussic acid of all things. None of us were surprised, he seemed the type. Always despairing of this or that. William Henry was rather the sort who would look down on shooting oneself, at least that is what I would have said before he did it."

"I had a similar feeling." Clara admitted, "But if he did not lock himself into a room and put a pistol to his head, we are left with the awful possibility of murder."

"That, oddly enough, would seem more likely to me!" Elijah laughed bleakly, "I could name you a fair few who would like to shoot him."

"Would you include yourself?"

Elijah was brought up short.

"Whatever reason could I have?"

"William Henry leaves no heir, and his only male relative, aside from you, is considerably aged. Eventually, after the death of Edward Sampford, you will inherit the family estate."

Elijah looked unimpressed.

"That is hardly something to kill for. The estate is in debt up to its crenelated turrets. It needs massive refurbishment work. Even if I sold it, I probably wouldn't have enough to pay off its debts. No, I am in no rush to gain that house. I hope Uncle Edward lives a very long time, long enough to have to deal with all those problems himself."

"There still might be worth in the land." Clara said, not convinced.

"Trust me, there isn't. Anyway, if you recall I was in the same room as your brother and Oliver Bankes when William Henry killed himself. That puts me out of the running for murderer."

"I suppose so." Clara was noncommittal, "What about last night? What can you remember before poor Simon Jones fell?"

"Well…" Elijah paused to recall the night before, "I was in bed around midnight, having danced over all those pots and pans of water Andrews put out. The captain was on watch at that point with that huge gun of his. I really didn't trust him with it. I climbed into bed. I was dog-tired and had drunk a fair amount of port. Amelia was raving next door, as usual. Not loudly, more under-her-breath, so I couldn't hear what she said, but it was annoying nonetheless. Despite that I did drift off to sleep, and then something woke me," Elijah tapped his finger on his lips as he tried to recall what had roused him, "It was before the bell rang. It was something like a door slamming, no, rather like a window slipping shut. I didn't really pay much attention. I turned over to go to sleep and it was a few minutes longer before I heard the bell begin to ring and then stop. I rolled onto my back, not sure I had really heard anything at all. Then I heard footsteps. Very soft. Then someone knocked a bowl over and it smashed. Someone ran past my door, must have been Jones. I jumped out of bed and threw back the door. I saw you, Oliver and the captain again. There was smashed porcelain all over the carpet but no sign of Simon Jones. Then there was the crash and, well…"

"Thank you Elijah, that has been most helpful." Clara said.

"I'm sorry about Simon. I feel bad about it since I asked Andrews and his team to investigate. Now this dreadful accident."

"You can't blame yourself."

"And auntie is so upset. I thought having other people in the house would help, rather it seems to have made things worse." Elijah groaned, "Why can't I ever do anything right?"

"It isn't your fault." Clara insisted quietly, "Mr Jones slipped, such things happen."

Elijah shut his eyes and looked miserable.

"I keep wondering, who will be next?"

"There will be no one else." Clara assured him.

"Really?" Elijah asked unconvinced.

"Really." Clara said firmly.

Chapter Seventeen

Clara was going to her room for a cardigan – she felt very cold – when she bumped into Oliver in the corridor. He was studying the big camera he had left set up ready to take a picture of the ghost. He looked up at Clara as she entered.

"I can't understand why it didn't go off." He motioned to the camera, "Or rather I can understand it, I just can't figure out how it happened."

Clara came over.

"How was it supposed to work?" She asked.

"Well, here is this cord, which is connected to the lens cap. When the cord is pulled the lens cap is jolted off and the camera can take a long exposure in the low light. To trigger the cord, it is attached to a tripwire of Andrews' design. Theoretically anyone snapping the tripwire would jerk the cord and remove the lens cap. We tested it countless times yesterday and it worked every time. Which is why I couldn't fathom that I had no picture this morning. Even if the ghost had not triggered it, Jones surely would have. So that is why I took a closer look."

Oliver pointed to the cord hanging from the lens cap. Clara followed his finger, tracing the cord with her eyes until she saw what had confused him so.

"It's been cut." She said.

"Precisely. It's been sabotaged."

"Hmm." Clara smiled, "If ever I needed proof to demonstrate this ghost was a real person, here it is."

"You think the ghost, or rather the person pretending to be the ghost, did this?"

"I would say more likely our ghost has an accomplice. This is intriguing. But who might it be?"

Oliver was still staring glumly at the camera cord.

"That puts paid to photographing a real ghost then." He sighed, "Even if I set it up without the camera being sabotaged, I'll only get a picture of a living person."

"Sorry to disappoint." Clara stared at his sad face and felt it summed up the feelings in the household, and that would just not do, especially at Christmas, "Look here Oliver, this whole house is down in the dumps. What do you say we attempt to give it a bit of Christmas cheer?"

Oliver looked at her curiously.

"I'm sure there are still some shops open. We'll get some holly and a wreath or two, and a tree. How can a house not have a tree at Christmas?" Clara was getting into full swing, "It's no good us all sitting around moping, particularly Miss Sampford, she looks quite frail suddenly. All this bad business has disturbed her and she needs something to brighten her up, else the ghost may just achieve its end after all."

"All right, you have me convinced." Oliver grinned.

"Good, you round up Tommy, I'll find Annie and we'll make a party of it."

She ushered Oliver off to the stairs and followed behind, feeling for the first time that week that she was taking charge of matters. Just as she was feeling quite jolly a sneeze overtook her and she had to blow her nose hard into her hanky. Damn cold, she puttered to herself, as she hastened downstairs.

~~*~~

It was just on midday when Miss Sampford opened her front door and was greeted with an array of green and red. Holly garlands decorated the bannisters of the stairs and mistletoe hung down from the lamp in the ceiling. Paper chains in rich gold and red shiny paper hung over the picture frames and a merry looking Father Christmas made of wax and dressed in real velvet stood on the hall stand. He beamed at Miss Sampford as his great sack of presents hung over his shoulder.

Humphry was standing in the centre of it all wearing a paper crown. Miss Sampford stared at him aghast.

"Your coat madam?" Humphry held out his arms to receive her outer wear.

"What do you have on your head, Humphry?" Miss Sampford asked, stifling a giggle.

"Miss Fitzgerald insisted." Humphry frowned, "Should I remove it?"

"No, it rather suits you." Miss Sampford handed him her coat, "Where is everyone?"

"In the dining room, madam."

Miss Sampford opened the door to her dining room and received her second surprise. A fire blazed heartily in the hearth, hanging above it were a series of stockings and more holly. In fact holly garlands decorated the entire room; around the mirror and paintings, sitting on the windowsills, there were even sprigs on the table, tucked among Christmas crackers and tiny golden reindeer that were frolicking among the cutlery. Yet, most impressive of all, was the huge fir tree sitting in the corner. It was adorned with candles and huge glass baubles, and right at the top an angel dressed in ivory silk. Miss Sampford stared and stared but she could not quite take in the sight of all the decorations.

"Do you approve?" Clara asked a tad nervously, coming alongside Miss Sampford, "I rather took it upon myself to make everything a bit more festive."

"Bless you." Miss Sampford said in a hushed tone. She pressed a hand to her lips as a small sob threatened to slip out, "Thank you Clara."

"No ghost is going to stop us enjoying Christmas." Clara winked at her.

Miss Sampford had to blink back tears.

"Now, I suggest we sit down for I know Mrs James has been working hard downstairs." Clara showed Miss Sampford to her seat and soon everyone was at the table, including Bridget Harper and Captain Adams. Clara felt it best everyone be present, which had meant insisting Amelia be coaxed out of her room by Elijah. She was sitting at her place looking very morose, but how else was one supposed to look after losing one's husband?

"You do have a flare for surprises Miss Fitzgerald." Edward Sampford said as he took his seat beside his wife, "It does look very nice, mind you."

"I made the paper chains." Elijah grinned at them all, "And mother said I learned nothing at university."

Humphry went about the table offering wine to the guests. A few moments later a bell rang and he hurried to open the dining room doors. There stood Mrs James proudly bearing a huge turkey on a platter. She was also wearing a paper crown. Behind her came Jane and Flo, each with serving bowls full of vegetables and stuffing balls. Mrs James set her turkey on the table and hurried to fetch the gravy while Humphry carved. Tommy started up a rousing rendition of Good King Wenceslas and soon most were joining in. By the time they had settled again each had a plate laden with food.

"I must say, this is one of the nicer Christmas days I have spent in a long time." Andrews said as he sliced into a roast parsnip, "Despite the events of last night."

A pall fell over the meal at the reminder of Simon Jones.

"Did he have family?" Miss Sampford asked with apprehension.

"No, he was a bachelor like myself." Andrews answered, "I suppose that was why we were able to devote so much energy to the pursuit of ghosts. Neither of us had any other constraints on our time."

"Does no one care about William Henry?" Amelia suddenly burst into the discussion, her face reddened with emotion, her lip trembling, "He was my family."

"Yes, my dear, we don't mean to dismiss your loss." Hilda Sampford stretched her hand out to Amelia, "We are just trying to make the best of things."

"Best? There is no 'best'. And that poor man last night." Amelia dug in a pocket for a handkerchief and dabbed at her eyes, "Something hideous is in this house."

"I am beginning to think it might be an Elemental." Andrews interjected, completely missing the tension suddenly fallen upon the table, "It would explain a lot."

"And what is an 'Elemental'?" Edward Sampford politely asked.

"An exact definition is hard to give, but many feel they are ancient forces, perhaps associated with the nature spirts our ancestors believed in. They have never existed as a person; rather they are a force or energy, stirred up usually by human activity. They can be harmless if left undisturbed, but aggressive when challenged."

"And they are dangerous?"

"Generally, yes." Andrews stated very matter-of-factly, "They can even be considered evil, but usually they will just wander about harming no one unless someone gets in their way."

"But, why does it keep trying to get into my room?" Miss Sampford said suddenly, "I am certain it has tried on more than one occasion. It is almost beyond what my nerves can bear."

"The whims of an Elemental are difficult to understand. Your room may just happen to be on the route it chooses to walk."

Clara found all her attention focused on Miss Sampford. The woman who, for a brief moment, had seemed lifted from her fears suddenly seemed to have shrunk and gone an awful grey colour. She no longer ate her food with pleasure, but picked at it miserably.

"Might I make a suggestion?" Clara asked.

"Go ahead," Miss Sampford answered quietly.

"Well, supposing we change bedrooms you and I. Your room is nearest the back stairs, mine is furthest away. I would be intrigued to see an Elemental, while you would be much happier in a non-haunted room."

"Thank you Clara, but I couldn't possibly impose."

"Nonsense." Clara insisted, "It will be my pleasure. You need a good night's sleep and I am perfectly capable of fending off a ghost."

"I would warn you, Elementals are dangerous." Andrews piped up. Clara ignored him.

"Well Miss Sampford?"

"It would be good to have a restful night." Miss Sampford agreed slowly, "But I would be mortified if anything were to happen to you Clara."

"Nothing will happen to me, of that I am certain." Clara smiled, "So it is agreed, we switch rooms?"

A little bit of colour returned to Miss Sampford's face.

"That sounds most agreeable."

At that moment the dining room doors burst open and Mrs James walked in bearing aloft a Christmas pudding haloed in whisky-fuelled flames. It was the biggest pudding Clara had seen in some time and there was a huge jug of brandy sauce to accompany it. Oliver grabbed a cracker off the table and waved it at Tommy. Tommy took the end and pulled, there was a bang and the guests cheered. Soon nearly everyone was pulling at their crackers and the room filled with booms and the strangely sulphuric smell of the explosive strip.

Clara nearly choked herself on her portion of Christmas pudding and spat out a small silver farthing. She examined it in the palm of her hand.

"It's good luck to find it." Miss Sampford smiled at her.

Clara had the overwhelming desire to hug the woman and tell her everything was going to be all right. Instead she put down the coin and smiled back. She would solve this mystery come what may.

After dinner the guests retired to the drawing room, where most either fell asleep in their chairs or smoked. Amelia disappeared to her room once more, not that anyone really noticed her going. Clara took Miss Sampford to one side so they could speak privately.

"I have a plan, Miss Sampford. Actually, I have already put it into action."

"Really?" Miss Sampford asked eagerly.

"I suggested we switch rooms over the dinner table so everyone would hear. You see, I am confident this ghost has an accomplice within your household, but rooting them out is more problematic."

"One of my guests?"

"I think so, but I can't be absolutely certain without laying a trap or two."

"And this is why you suggested switching rooms?" Miss Sampford clarified.

"Yes, you see, by saying about us switching rooms out loud, if there is an accomplice in this house they now know you will not be in your own room tonight. If the ghost, therefore, wishes to seek you out, they must go to a different room and if they do that then once and for all we know this ghost is a living person who had an accomplice sitting around the dinner table."

"And if they don't, if they still come to my old room you will be convinced they are a ghost?"

"Or that their accomplice was not at dinner. Do you understand my logic?"

"I do, but should you be right about this ghost being a living person I will still be in danger?" Miss Sampford went pale.

"Absolutely not." Clara assured her, "Because we are not actually going to change rooms, only appear to. You will sleep in your own room and Annie will stay with you. In that way you only have to fear a silly old ghost. On the other hand I will be ready and waiting for any person headed your way."

"It's all so risky Clara."

"Don't worry about me. It is you I am concerned with. We have had two deaths in this household in the space of two days. I don't intend to let this mischief continue."

Miss Sampford suddenly felt a tad faint and had to lean back against an occasional table to keep her balance.

"I just don't understand why this ghost continues to haunt my home with everyone around. If it is a living person, surely they would have the sense to avoid the house while I have ghost hunters and detectives in residence?"

"But then we would know at once that the ghost was a real person. If we accept such a thing as ghosts, we should also accept that they have no interest or concerns about ghost hunters or the like. Should your ghost suddenly vanish with the arrival of people, then that would imply it had some sort of consciousness and did not want to be seen. And only living, breathing people react in such ways. Whoever is behind this crime does not want people to start imagining the ghost is a fabrication, it scuppers their entire plan, whether that be to scare you from your home or worse. Therefore they have to keep putting on the performance, or else raise suspicions that the ghost isn't genuine."

"That is surely so risky?" Miss Sampford said.

"Yes, but supposing they could convinced Mr Andrews there really was a ghost. Then it would be fixed in peoples' minds that the property was haunted and should anything happen to you it might be looked upon as the actions of a ghost rather than a living murderer."

Miss Sampford nodded sadly.

"Should I die of fright, peoples' first thoughts will be of the ghost."

"I believe that is the gamble the ghost is taking." What Clara didn't voice out loud was that she also suspected the perpetrators of this hoax were running out of time. They had already upped the ante by pushing Simon Jones downstairs, now they were no doubt panicking. Whatever their ultimate goal it had to be achieved soon, before anyone began to get too suspicious about a man falling down a set of stairs.

"I must admit I am dreading everyone going home. The house will be so empty again. Please solve this mystery before that happens."

"I promise Miss Sampford. I'm going to nab this ghost."

Miss Sampford gently smiled.

"I remember once being like you, young and full of confidence. How did I let it all slip away?"

"I don't think you have." Clara answered with certainty.

Chapter Eighteen

That night Clara and Miss Sampford went through the motions of switching rooms. Jane and Flo transferred boxes and belongings, changed bed linen and stoked the fires. Then, when all the other guests were tucked up in their rooms, Clara and Miss Sampford once more switched places. Annie gave Clara a hug and a kiss before she followed Miss Sampford to her room.

"Take care Clara."

"Ghosts don't scare me Annie."

Annie pulled a face.

"They scare me."

Clara was unperturbed. She doubted she would even notice a ghost should one come prowling. She felt utterly exhausted and full of the chills and flushes of a good head cold. She dressed in her warmest nightgown and wrapped a scarf about her neck for extra warmth, before climbing beneath the blankets. Somewhere a church bell rang and carol singers circled the Square giving a stirring – if off-key – rendition of We Three Kings. Clara listened to them until some irate householder yelled at them to be quiet and threatened to summon the police. There was a slight commotion as the carollers responded in kind with a few choice words and the soft thud of thrown snowballs, and then there was another yell and the sound of running feet. Clara sighed; yes, the Christmas spirit was alive and well.

The house fell into peace and quiet. The fire waned down to soft embers and the room fell still. Clara listened to her own breathing and the first wet patters of a fresh fall of snow. Silence, deep dark silence. The minutes ticked by on the face of an old mantel clock. Clara pulled the blankets further up to her nose. She wanted to fall asleep but a part of her resisted, she realised she had lied to Annie – she was a little scared.

Then, there it was. The faintest of creaks as the far door of the back stairs opened. No one was on watch in the hall tonight, a good feast and plenty of wine and whisky had made even the usually alert Andrews hanker for his bed. But the tripwires and trickery were all present. Clara waited for the far bell to tinkle; it didn't, a hand had reached out and stopped it while the wire was safely cut. Clara had no doubt that the camera had also been sabotaged as before, which was why she had suggested Oliver remove the lens cap right before he went to bed, but leave the cord in a position that made it seem as if the lens cap was still in place. In the dim light the camera would take an extremely long exposition and it might, with any luck, catch something. It all depended, Oliver had said, they might get nothing but a blank plate. But if they did get a picture... well, then Clara might have yet another clue to expose the person behind this prank.

She lay still. Footsteps fell on the floor very quietly, very stealthily. Every now and then there was a pause and Clara suspected this was to negotiate the numerous tripwires Andrews had placed. Again these were not the actions of an ethereal being.

The footsteps came closer. Clara judged they had gone past Miss Sampford's room and were now heading towards her own. So there had been an accomplice at the dinner table and they had informed the 'ghost' of the switched bedrooms. Clara pulled herself up a little in bed.

She had left the curtains drawn back on the windows to allow in the moonlight. The room was relatively bright as the snow reflected the opalescent starlight. The footsteps had come to Clara's door. The handle creaked tentatively under a hand. Clara had chosen not to make life easy for the ghost and had locked her door. When the handle resisted against the lock there was a pause, then a scrape of metal. Someone on the other side had placed a key into the lock.

Clara held her breath. The key turned. The tumblers of the lock clicked and the handle once again twisted beneath murderous fingers. The door groaned open, the tip of a foot was visible, and a veiled head. The figure ducked into the room and Clara realised it was a woman wearing an old-fashioned dress, the sort her grandmother used to wear with large full skirts and a nipped waist. The figure was dressed all in black. The veil hung completely over her head and revealed nothing. The mysterious woman pushed the door closed behind her and approached the bed with cautious steps.

Clara pretended to be asleep and breathing deeply, but her eyes were open just enough to watch the figure's movement. As the veiled woman reached the side of the bed, her other hand came from behind her back holding a long, thin knife that caught the moonlight and sparkled. The woman leaned over Clara, her arm raised; there was no doubt what she intended to do. As the knife flew down Clara rolled to her left, the blade ripping the blankets but missing her entirely. Before the mystery woman could recover Clara lunged at her and grabbed the arm with the knife. They wrestled, the veiled figure proving remarkably strong as she dug her fingernails into Clara's wrists. Clara started to shout out for help and the mystery woman panicked. She let go of the knife and threw herself backwards, dragging Clara completely over the bed and sending her toppling to the floor. In the fall Clara let go her grasp to prevent her face smashing nose-first into the floor, and the momentary release allowed the veiled woman to dash for the door.

Clara was on her feet in an instant and running after her. The woman was already through the door and heading for the main stairs. Clara chased her, going so fast she didn't see the tripwire Andrews had laid where the corridor met the landing. She caught her foot and went down hard on her elbows. She was stunned for a moment and when she regained her feet the woman was already racing down the next set of stairs. Clara followed, hobbling slightly on the foot she had caught. On the ground floor the front door was standing wide open and nothing but a faint trail of footsteps in the snow indicated where the woman had gone.

Clara ran into the Square, the cold biting through her gown and her feet burning on the icy snow. The footsteps left the path and hastened into the road where a day's worth of traffic had cleared most of the snow. After that they were lost. Clara stood and stared into the darkness, turning left and right to try and see the veiled woman, but she was gone, vanished into the dark. Shivering, Clara abandoned the chase and headed back indoors, cursing Andrews and her own clumsiness.

She had just shut the front door when Oliver and Elijah came hurrying down the stairs.

"What happened?" Oliver asked.

"The ghost." Clara said as she put the bolt across on the door, "She came into my room."

"She?" Elijah asked incredulously.

"It was wearing a dress." Clara shrugged.

"And you chased her?" Oliver motioned to the door.

"As best I could, come look at this." Clara led them back upstairs and to her room. She quickly lit a candle and then walked over to where the knife still lay on the floor, "She lost it in the struggle."

Oliver was silent, but Elijah gave a pained squeak.

"She was intent on murder." Clara clarified, "Naturally she thought I was Miss Sampford after our conversation over switching rooms."

"Oh Clara." Oliver suddenly came over and hugged her, "I'm glad you are all right."

"But… my aunt…" Elijah looked a little sick, "Who is behind this?"

"Someone in this house who has access to keys and can unlock the front door for our felon. That also explains why the activity has increased over Christmas. The murderer could not make their move until their accomplice was installed in the house. That probably rules you out Elijah."

"Thanks." Elijah remarked bitterly, "Will she come back?"

"Not tonight." Clara said, though she had to admit to herself she was not entirely confident of that. The ghost now knew it had been rumbled and would probably become more desperate to attain its end.

"But the accomplice is still here." Oliver added, "Clara, I won't have you sleeping alone in a room with a murderer on the loose."

"Honestly, Oliver…"

"No, I insist, where is Annie?"

"Watching over Miss Sampford and there she will remain, I'm more worried about that poor woman than myself."

"Then I shall camp out in your dressing room for the night." Oliver said stoutly, "For your own protection."

Clara rolled her eyes.

"That is completely unnecessary."

"I think not, I shall fetch my blanket and my dressing gown and shall be ready for action at the slightest disturbance." It was quite clear Oliver would not be moved from acting the role of heroic protector. Clara conceded, she felt too tired and ill to argue.

Oliver left to fetch his blankets and Elijah was alone in the room with Clara.

"I never thought…" Elijah was in a daze, staring aghast at the knife, "You must believe me, I honestly thought this was a genuine ghost."

"I do believe you Elijah." Clara assured him as she went to sit on the edge of her bed.

"I can't believe anyone would want to hurt my aunt. She has done no harm to anyone."

"Sometimes we do harm without even knowing it." Clara shrugged, "And then again some people are just wicked."

"This is about money, isn't it?"

"Maybe."

"Tomorrow I shall insist all the keys in the house are collected and handed over to Humphry for safekeeping, only my aunt shall be allowed one for her room, then this vile creature cannot creep in undetected." Elijah paused, "Unless you think Humphry is the accomplice?"

"I don't think that. He has been with your aunt a long time, besides he would not need to wait until so many guests were here to enact his plan. He could have done it anytime when there were far fewer witnesses to notice."

Elijah nodded.

"Yes, I see that." His eyes were still on the knife, "Does this mean Simon Jones was murdered?"

"I suspect so. He probably chased the ghost and realised, like I did, that she was a real person. The only option the murderer had then, if she wished to continue her plan, was to push him to his death and hope everyone would think it an accident."

"And my cousin?"

Clara said nothing for a moment.

"I can't decide on that one. Everything points to it being suicide, but without a real reason for his death I can't be certain. I don't suppose you ever saw him in London, did you?"

"No." Elijah said, but there was something in his tone that made Clara look at him hard.

"But perhaps you had heard rumours?"

Elijah bit his lip.

"Your aunt is in a lot of danger, now is not the time to be coy." Clara reminded him.

"It was only talk." Elijah said unhappily, "Some of the fellows at university are… experimental. One time I heard them mention my cousin's name. I was surprised how they knew him and they said certain people knew William extremely well. It took me a while to understand what they meant."

"I don't suppose you could put me in touch with these fellows?"

Elijah grimaced.

"The scandal…"

"Elijah, I am discreet, but I can't tiptoe around when your aunt is in danger. If William Henry's death is connected or if it is not, it is important I find out. Equally, if his death was not suicide I can't leave the matter unresolved."

"Let me think about it." Elijah ducked the issue, "I… I should get back to bed."

He left the room just as Oliver returned. He was carrying blankets, pillows, an oil lamp, candle, and a length of curtain cord. Clara looked at him curiously.

"In case she comes back and we need to tie her up." He informed her, "Also I went and took the camera down and replaced the lens cap. Just in case we got a picture, don't need it ruined by over-exposure."

"Are you sure you are sufficiently prepared?" Clara asked as straight-faced as she could manage.

Oliver looked at his bundles.

"I think so. Should I borrow the colonel's shotgun?"

"Hm, no." Clara started to crawl back into bed.

Oliver made his way to the dressing room and for a time could be heard arranging his bedding. Then all was quiet. Clara rested her head back on her pillow and tried to clear her mind. She wanted to preserve the image of the woman she had seen as precisely as she could manage. The face had been obscured, but she could garner some details. She was about five foot, for a start, shorter than Clara and her hands had been pale and smooth, not the hands of an old person. Her dress was curious, but then if you were pretending to be a ghost, Clara supposed, it was prudent to dress in old-fashioned costume. And she had been wearing a faint scent – Clara tried to focus her mind on the aroma. She had smelt it before, but exactly where would not come to her. It was a floral scent, not overly heavy and rather like roses, but with a hint of something else. Perhaps it would prove important. Clara did her best to fix all these minor details in her mind before sleep over-took her and she finally got some much needed rest.

Chapter Nineteen

Clara rose late. Annie had dropped into her room around seven and been startled by the sight of Oliver sprawled across the bed in the dressing room. She had given him a sound poke and when he opened his eyes she insisted he explain everything. Which is exactly what he did, leaving Annie feeling very worried. After she had quietly and discreetly shuffled him out of Clara's room she returned, stoked the fire, and then left her friend to rest.

When Clara finally roused from a deep and comforting sleep it was close to ten o'clock in the morning and most of the household had been awake for a couple of hours. Admittedly several of them were feeling a little worse for wear from the night before and not exactly bright-eyed and bushy-tailed. Clara sat up in bed and a piece of paper slipped off the covers onto the floor. She leaned down and retrieved it. It was a blurry photograph, showing the ill-lit corridor and a vacuous, fuzzy figure walking down it. The experiment with the long exposure had been a partial success; they had caught an image of someone, it just wasn't clear enough to make an identification. Clara slipped the photograph into a bedside drawer, sneezed, and started to get dressed. She needed a strong cup of tea and time to think.

Downstairs in the dining room people were still eating breakfast. Andrews was attempting to master a plate of black pudding and eggs, insisting to a grimacing Bridget Harper that this was a certain cure for a hangover. Clara helped herself to kedgeree and sat quietly at the far end of the table, yawning as she forked up rice.

"Our ghost came again last night." Andrews announced down the table, a little too brightly for his own good. He pressed a hand to his forehead.

"Did they?" Clara said innocently.

"Several tripwires broken, but several others intact. Typical behaviour for an Elemental."

Clara merely nodded.

"Miss Sampford didn't hear anything. Did you?"

"No." Clara lied.

"Humph." Andrews muttered, "As I should expect, women sleep so heavily."

Bridget Harper gave him a scowl.

"This arrived for you madam." Humphry placed a parcel on the table in front of Clara.

"How odd, who knows I am here?" She pulled at the parcel string and the brown paper flopped open to reveal a Christmas card and a key.

Clara picked up the card which showed a rather gauche picture of the Nativity and flipped it open.

Dear Miss Fitzgerald, read the contents, I must apologise for my earlier abruptness, I misunderstood your intentions. My man returned on Christmas Eve and told me of your kindness towards him. I found myself regretting the subterfuge I had orchestrated. Thank you for being so forgiving and please accept this gift as a token of my profuse apologies. I am sure you appreciate its significance.

Season's Greetings
John Mollinson.

Clara turned her attention to the key and smiled. Now she had access to No.49 and one mystery might just be solved – how was the perpetrator of the ghost getting into a locked house? Now there was an accomplice on the premises that could be answered simply enough, but before that? Aside from Miss Sampford the only people who had been inside the property the entire time of the haunting were Humphry and Mrs James. Clara was reluctant to blame either servant, they both seemed too dedicated to their mistress to want to plot her death. In any case, she was confident the accomplice had arrived with the Christmas guests.

Clara put down the card and gave no further sign of her excitement. She did not want the whole house knowing what she had in her hand.

"From an admirer, Clara?" Miss Sampford asked.

"From a friend." Clara answered, "I met them on my second day here and completely forgot I had mentioned I was staying in Berkeley Square. People are so kind, I must respond at once."

"What is that in the parcel?" Bridget Harper spoke with unprecedented curiosity.

"A card." Clara said, pretending she misunderstood, then hurried from the table muttering about finding somewhere still stocking Christmas cards this late in the season.

A short time later she was letting herself into No. 49. The house was empty, as was to be expected, but smelt of new paint and wood. Clara let the door close behind her and locked it. She doubted the 'ghost' spent all her time in the property, too risky after all with the random visits of workmen, so she was confident she had the place to herself. Clara rubbed her gloved hands together and prepared for a thorough inspection of the premises.

No.49 was built on a mirror image version of the floor plan as No.50, this intrigued Clara as it meant the ghost could spend as much time in No.49 as she wanted, plotting the best routes around the neighbouring No.50 without setting foot into the actual house. It didn't take Clara long to become convinced that there had to be a secret passage between the two, but try as she might she could not find it. No sliding panel, no spring-loaded door, nothing, in fact, in any way reminiscent of the adventure stories she had read as a child. Clara had to conclude the back stairs were not the answer.

She went for a wander about the rest of the house. Mollinson's alterations to make the property more suitable as a hotel were apparent. The dining room had been extended into the back room to make enough space for all the guests and the snug and drawing room had been merged into one and the first trappings of a lobby were being installed. In the basement the many small servant rooms were being knocked around to make larger spaces and to increase the size of the kitchen. The rubble still present on the floor suggested to Clara this was very much a work in progress. On the first and second floors the bedrooms had been stripped to the bone and Clara noted the carpentry work on the floor. The watchman in the park had been correct when he said he had had to replace a large number of boards.

Finally Clara found herself on the third floor, feeling that her excitement had been unwarranted. The house provided no further clues whatsoever. But, to be certain, she set out to explore the last few rooms. The builders had not yet made it to the third floor and the original wallpaper still hung on the walls showing the stains of many years. Clara found the rooms in surprisingly poor repair. The previous owner had presumably not needed to use them and had allowed them to simply rot away. In one there was even a blackbird perched on top of a long forgotten dressing table. The blackbird shrieked at her vocally before flying straight out the window. Clara was startled for an instant, until she realised the window contained no glass.

How odd, Clara mused to herself. Presumably the window had been broken, the glass removed and never replaced. With the door shut no one would notice the missing window until they reached this room, and with no heating in the place it was hardly likely anyone would notice the cold. Then Clara began to wonder, could this be what she had been searching for?

Clara peered out the window. It was a long drop down, but what intrigued her was the ledge that ran beneath the window. It was barely the width of a foot, but it ran all the way across to No.50 as part of the decoration. Clara examined it while the cold winter wind blew in her face, supposing - just supposing – one of the windows in No. 50 was a tad loose? What Clara contemplated next had never before crossed her mind. She reached out and felt the ledge. Considering the snowfall overnight the ledge was suspiciously clear. There was nothing for it but to take a chance.

Clara eased herself out the window, gripping onto the frame and putting her left foot over the sill first, then she stretched out the right. Gingerly she pulled herself upright, trying not to look down. The view was admittedly impressive, she could see into the windows and gardens of all the houses that backed on to those of Berkeley Square. She just hoped nobody was staring back at her. With trepidation she slid one foot along the ledge, then the other. Slowly, a fraction at a time, she moved away from the window. The wind whipped around her and the feeling of being virtually walking on thin air was horrible. For a moment she almost went back, but if she wanted to prove this was the way the ghost was sneaking into No.50 then she had to carry on. Hoping that Georgian architecture was as sturdy as it looked she edged onwards, her fingers clinging to the brickwork, her stomach turning over. About halfway she heard a small voice.

"Cor lummy, Joe, look there!" Clara dared to peek in the direction of the voice and spotted a small boy in the alley that ran beside No.50. He was carrying a basket and appeared to be making a delivery. An older boy stood next to him.

"She's cooked!" This lad, presumably Joe, announced in a voice laden with disapproval.

Clara tried to ignore them.

"Miss! Miss! What are you doing miss?" The younger lad called out.

"I've misplaced my key." Clara called back.

The boys contemplated this for a moment before coming to the conclusion that no one climbs to the third floor of a building and balances on a ledge because they have lost their key.

"Want us to ring the front bell?" Joe said in the same unsympathetic tone.

"Really I rather you wouldn't, I am almost there." Clara responded, in fact she was now level with the first window on the third floor of No.50. She tried to lift it, but it failed to move.

"Are you a burglar?" The young boy piped up.

"Does she look like a burglar Sam?" Joe gave his comrade a shove.

"Then why is she up there?" Sam replied with infallible logic.

"Look, if I tell you, you won't believe me." Clara said, inching her way to the next window, at least the boys were distracting her from the drop below, "I assure you it is nothing illegal."

"So what is it?" Joe demanded, folding his arms across his chest and looking like a very stern schoolmaster.

Clara couldn't believe she was attempting to explain herself to two children.

"I am conducting an experiment to see if it is possible to climb from a window of No.49 to a window of No.50."

"Why?" Sam asked.

"Well, because someone has been sneaking into this house and I want to know how they have been doing it."

"Sounds fishy to me." Joe squinted up at Clara, "Come on Sam, let's ring the bell and tell 'em they have a burglar trying to break in."

"You said she weren't a burglar!"

"Don't argue Sam, just follow me!" The boys legged it back down the alley to the front of the house.

Clara was relieved they were gone, but had no intention of being discovered clinging to the outside of the house. She was now level with the room where William Henry had met his end and was beginning to wonder why she had ever considered this a viable route into the house at all. She got hold of the sash window, expecting it to be locked like all the others when, remarkably, it opened. Clara stared at the raised window, but only for a moment as she had no desire to loiter on a ledge for any longer than necessary. Holding onto the frame she slipped her legs inside and descended into the room. Then she quietly lowered the window until it was shut.

By the time the boys returned with Humphry there was no sign of Clara, and he gave them both a cuff round the ear for wasting his time.

Clara stood in the room where William Henry had breathed his last and realised she now had evidence that it was possible (just possible) that he had not, in fact, shot himself. She went to the door and was relieved to find it was unlocked. So here was how the ghost had snuck in and out. William Henry had stumbled across her, perhaps, and found his fate sealed. It wouldn't surprise Clara either if the ghost had a key to the room, after all, she had had a key to Clara's.

A thought suddenly struck her. She slipped down the stairs as silently as she could and back out the front door. In the street she hastened to No.49, passing the same boys that had been in the alley.

"There she is, look, making a getaway!" Cried Sam.

The boys ran after Clara as she thudded into the door of No.49 completely forgetting she had locked it.

"Oh bother!"

"What is she doing now Joe?" Sam queried his friend.

"Surely it is obvious I have locked myself out?" Clara announced to them, "I completely forgot I had locked the door when I climbed out the window, and I am certainly not going to climb back that way."

Joe and Sam gave her strange looks, trying to fathom what this bizarre woman was about.

"Why do you want to go in there?" Joe asked suspiciously.

Clara sighed and perched against the railing that ran up to the door."

"You two look like smart lads." She said conversationally, "I am sure you have heard about the ghost at No.50?"

The boys nodded eagerly.

"Well," Said Clara, "I am on the trail of the ghost. I know she comes from No.49 and I was exploring about to see if I could find proof. That's why I climbed out the window, I think that is how she gets from this house to next door."

"You're a ghost hunter!" Sam asked with obvious glee.

"Does Mr Mollinson know about this?" Joe was still looking at her as if she was a common criminal. Clara knew a fellow cynic when she saw one.

"Yes, he gave me the key for the house. Here." Clara handed over the Christmas car from Mollinson which she had kept in her pocket to avoid it falling into the wrong hands, "And now I have left his key inside. It is very awkward, I shall have to call a locksmith."

"No you won't." Joe handed back the card with a sigh that suggested what he was about to do was against his better judgement, "I have a key for the back door."

He produced a brass key from his pocket.

"We deliver milk and bread and cheese here every day for the workmen." Sam helpfully explained, "Sometimes we get here when they aren't around so Mr Mollinson gave our boss a key. Joe looks after it. We have to give it back when Mr Mollinson says, though."

Clara smiled at them.

"I am jolly glad you two spotted me."

"I ain't." Joe rubbed at his ear.

Joe led the way round the back and let Clara in. The two lads waited outside, insisting they were only allowed as far as the kitchen and no further. Clara fetched the key from the front door and then went to the third floor and removed a bedroom door key. She returned to Joe and Sam.

"Thanks lads, will you come have some of the finest Christmas cake around?"

Sam looked at Joe, clearly the leader in this little partnership. Joe shrugged.

"Suppose."

Clara took them into the kitchen at No.50 and asked Annie to cut two big slices of cake for her wonderful helpers.

"You look pleased with yourself, Clara." Annie said, as she fetched some of her Christmas cake for the boys.

"I think I am finally getting to the bottom of this ghost business." Clara grinned.

Humphry appeared at the door of the kitchen, having come to fetch tea for Miss Sampford and stared at the two boys. A modicum of surprise almost slipped through his façade of disinterest.

"That's the lady who was climbing about outside." Sam pointed at Clara, Christmas cake falling from his mouth, "We weren't lying!"

Humphry stared at Clara, one eyebrow lifted in a questioning manner.

"It is quite true Humphry I have been climbing the masonry." Clara said, "It's all to help keep Miss Sampford safe, however."

"Jolly good madam." Humphry picked up the tray of tea and left without another word.

"He could have apologised." Sam said, but the pang of righteous annoyance lasted mere moments before he returned to his cake.

Annie shook her head at Clara.

"Corrupting the young now, are we?"

"Are you implying I am a bad influence?" Clara looked hurt.

"I'm not implying." Annie said with crossed arms, "I'm telling you."

Chapter Twenty

Clara decided it was time she had a long talk with Miss Sampford. As much as she liked the woman, she couldn't shake the feeling there was something – or rather someone – in her past that she was refusing to talk about. There was a reason for this whole ghost performance and with William Henry out of the picture Clara was growing increasingly unconvinced about money being the motive. William Henry's death on its own was puzzling, was it by accident or design? Murder or suicide? She could not yet rule out either.

She found Miss Sampford in her snug, carefully collecting up her Christmas cards and making a note of all those who had sent her one for the following year's Christmas card list.

"Dear Clara, do people still make Christmas card lists? Elijah says I am an old fuss-pot over it. He can't fathom why I still send cards to people I have not seen in years. Take this one," Miss Sampford held up a card featuring a strangely summery scene of the Nativity, "this comes from an old friend now residing in South Africa. She and her husband breed cattle of some native type. She went out there in 1872. Heavens, I don't suppose we would even recognise each other now, but we always send Christmas cards every year."

Miss Sampford sighed.

"It is somewhat of a strain these days. Waiting to see who sends one a card and who cannot because they have passed on into the dreamy yonder. I am missing two this year and I dare say I shall have a letter in the January post responding to the cards I sent them, explaining they are no longer with us."

She placed the cards on a side table, it was still a bulging pile despite Miss Sampford's claims that her circle of friends was diminishing rapidly.

"I dare say there are perhaps one or two cards waiting on the doormat at home." Clara said, fingering one topmost card featuring a plump robin surrounded by snow, "I'm a terrible correspondent."

"You must have friends, Clara?" Miss Sampford said in surprise.

"Oh yes, but only a handful really. I just seem too busy all the time for socialising. I suppose I could have kept in touch with all the girls at school, but somehow, once I was away from them, I just couldn't be bothered." Clara frowned, "I think perhaps I am a little too blunt for most people and not everyone wants to be associated with a female private detective."

"I think you are wonderfully refreshing." Miss Sampford said with the first smile Clara had seen on her face that day, "You call a spade a spade. My, you would have made a grand suffragette!"

"I fear I am too lazy when it comes to politics." Clara responded.

"My dear, I think you are anything but lazy. Now, why have you come searching for me? You have been bustling about these last two days with a clear plan in mind, now I fear you want to talk to me about something important?"

Clara gave an apologetic look and sat down.

"I now know for certain your ghost is as flesh and blood as you or I." She said.

Miss Sampford went pale.

"Oddly, I dreaded that more than you discovering we had a dangerous spectre in the house. How did you make your discovery?"

"I won't trouble you with the mundane details, but I have learned how the ghost is entering and leaving the building, also I had the opportunity to chase her last night."

"Her?"

"Yes."

Miss Sampford fell silent. Her eyes wandered to the teetering pile of cards.

"Did she kill William Henry?"

"Maybe."

Miss Sampford made a strange gulping noise and looked half-choked by her emotions.

"And Mr Jones?"

Clara hesitated, but there was really no point, the woman had already guessed what she had tried to hide.

"I can't say for certain because there were no witnesses, but it is probable he was pushed down the stairs once he realised the ghost was very much a living person." Clara said.

"Mr Andrews will be disappointed." Miss Sampford made an attempt to lighten the mood with humour, but it failed to work, "What now Clara?"

"Miss Sampford, I must know, why is this person after you? I'm not convinced this is about money or your nephew. It feels like something else, something more personal."

"I really don't know Clara." Miss Sampford answered, raising her hands gently in apology.

"Think back, is there anyone you have upset, not necessarily on purpose but by the misfortune of circumstances?"

"Really Clara, I am not the sort to bear grudges or make enemies. I admit my suffrage days were different and I ruffled a few feathers. But almost always male feathers, so how this woman would fit in I can't imagine. Besides, that was such an age ago."

"Have you ever dismissed a servant, perhaps?"

"Mrs James hires the maids and deals with them as she sees fit. I've never had complaint."

"There must be someone."

"Clara, I am just not the sort of person who has problems like you describe. I have no idea of anyone who might have a complaint against me."

Clara was growing frustrated because she was convinced she was being lied to.

"Even the most innocuous of people has an enemy. They may not be of their own creating even. People take up grudges for the oddest of reasons." She stated, prodding the issue.

"There is simply no one." Miss Sampford insisted, "Except those I have already mentioned. I cannot help you further Clara."

"All right." Clara conceded defeat for the time being, "Then let's turn our minds to how we are going to nab this 'ghost'."

"Nab?" Miss Sampford raised her eyebrows.

"Catch. Bring to justice." Clara explained, "Without knowing her motive or even a possible identity, it is impossible for me to try hunting her down in the streets. So we must set a trap and hope to snare her in it."

"Oh dear, I have a nasty feeling you are going to tell me I am the bait." Miss Sampford winced.

"I'm afraid so. The ghost has clearly become bolder since the arrival of your guests. Among them is the ghost's accomplice who is feeding her information. What we need is to feed her the right information that forces her to act recklessly, thus we are the ones who have the advantage."

"You have a plan?"

"The ghost is running out of time to finish her work. I suspect it was always intended that she would strike once your house was full of guests and her accomplice was in place. Before then it was too dangerous, but after the house was full there would be so many suspects that the police would have their hands full dealing with them all. Hopefully, following the initial confusion, the accomplice would emerge unscathed and the incident would be labelled as yet another of life's mysteries." Clara wished there was an easier way to explain all this, "Any practical policeman would dismiss tales of ghosts for what they were and so the real culprit would disappear in the confusion."

"How horrible." Miss Sampford said quietly, "So what am I to do?"

"I want you to announce to your guests that you have decided to bring an end to the Christmas festivities. Make whatever apologies and excuses you feel necessary. Explain that you want everyone to go home tomorrow. The ghost will thus be forced to act before her accomplice disappears."

Miss Sampford looked aghast.

"I can't possibly turn away my guests like that!"

"It is necessary to lure out the ghost."

Miss Sampford was displeased.

"It is simply not done. To tell my brother to leave? To inform Elijah and Amelia to pack up and go? To chase off those silly ghost hunters... well, that I don't mind, but I have never ended Christmas early and I can't imagine starting now."

"You can explain the truth to them as soon as the ghost is caught." Clara tried to mollify her.

"It simply won't do!"

"Please Miss Sampford." Clara begged, "It really is necessary."

Miss Sampford looked at Clara very sternly, then her expression softened.

"I shall agree to a compromise."

"Which is?"

"You, Clara, shall spread the rumour that this episode has so unsettled my nerves that I am considering sending my guests away so I might have some peace to recover. I shall say nothing but, if your ghost is as desperate as you fear, even just the threat of my sending everyone away will be enough to rout them."

Clara thought that her original plan had a better chance of success, but she was prepared to compromise since there seemed little chance of persuading Miss Sampford to make the announcement herself.

"Very well. I shall begin to spread my rumours."

"Thank you Clara." Miss Sampford said, but there was a tension in her demeanour, as though despite her denials Clara had shaken some thought, some suspicion, loose within her, "I shall get back to my Christmas cards."

Clara knew when she was being dismissed and left the snug to put her plan into action. Almost at once she bumped into Elijah who was coming down the stairs.

"Miss Fitzgerald." He held out a note to her, "Those names we discussed."

"Thank you." Clara took the piece of paper without looking at it, "I've just been speaking with your aunt, the events of the last few days have shaken her considerably."

"No doubt." Elijah concurred.

"She is wondering whether to send all her guests home, yourself included, so she can attempt to recover in peace."

Elijah looked genuinely startled.

"By Jove, I didn't realise things were so bad. But would she really want to be left alone with that thing on the loose?"

"Your aunt is of the opinion the ghost is nothing more than a figment of her imagination." Clara lied smoothly, "And this has led two men to their deaths, or so she imagines in her mind. Without frightening her with the full details of what we witnessed last night I cannot convince her otherwise, and I don't think it would be sensible to upset her so."

"Quite." Elijah pulled a pained face, "We've got to do something Clara!"

"I quite agree, but right now I am not sure what. Don't think I will leave your aunt in danger, however."

"Nor will I!" Elijah declared stoutly, "I saw that bloody vicious knife last night. The thought of it going into my aunt makes me shiver. I'll protect her even if I am the only person in the house left to do so."

Clara patted his shoulder.

"Let's hope it doesn't come to that."

Slipping the note in her pocket she went in search of Amelia Sampford; better to deal with the scary one first. Amelia was not so hard to find as she spent most of her time in her room. Out of all the guests in the house Clara imagined she would be the only one glad to leave. She had not ruled her out as a suspect, however. Perhaps she was in on a plot with William Henry?

Clara knocked on Amelia's door.

"Who is it?"

"Miss Fitzgerald, might we speak?"

"Go away!"

Clara had expected as much.

"We perhaps got off on the wrong foot. I am terribly sorry for your loss and would like to make amends for our problematic introduction." She suggested diplomatically.

"We are hardly destined to be bosom friends." Amelia snapped sarcastically.

"Indeed." Clara admitted, "I just thought you might appreciate someone to talk to, someone who is separate from your family."

"No!" Amelia snapped.

There was a strange noise in the room. A fluttering sound, followed by a thump as if something had been thrown.

"Damn thing, get out! Get out!" Amelia started to shriek and now there was the sound of someone tearing about the room.

"Amelia? What is it?" Clara had visions of a banshee-like woman chasing Amelia around the room with a knife, "Are you in trouble? Please open the door!"

"Get it away! Away!"

Clara could wait no longer, she still had the bedroom key from No.49. She put it in the lock and turned it. The door, as she had suspected, unlocked and she was able to enter the room. Her brief satisfaction that she had proved another element of the ghost story – how the wraith had managed to open locked doors – quickly evaporated as she raced in to help Amelia.

To her surprise the room was deserted, aside from the frightened cowering woman sitting in a corner and batting at something invisible.

"Get it away!" She kept crying out.

Clara approached her cautiously.

"What is it Amelia?" Clara asked, watching as the woman struck out again and again with her hands.

"Birds, fluttering birds, they keep coming. I open the window to let them out but they won't go!"

Clara crouched down carefully before Amelia.

"How long have you seen the birds Amelia?"

"Always." Amelia sniffed, her flailing hand movements slowing down, "Always. But William made them go away."

"How did he make them go away?" Clara didn't dare get too close and startle the woman who was clearly mad.

"I don't know. Some blue stuff, in a bottle. He said it made me free of the birds."

Clara stood and looked about the room. She realised she was looking for some sort of medicine that William Henry had kept sole charge of. With him gone, Amelia had reverted to whatever strange chaos her mind naturally resided in. But the bottle had to be near. Clara went to a trunk and opened it, looking for something that looked like a medicine chest. When that failed she went to William Henry's shaving kit which was in a large upright box and included several bottles of cologne and tooth powders. Among them all was a small blue bottle with a carefully printed label. Clara picked it up and read the name of a doctor on the label, before looking at the list of ingredients. These included cocaine, morphia, ether and alcohol, along with some smaller quantities of drugs she was unfamiliar with. A warning label stated that the patient should take no more than two drops mixed in a glass of water. Clara had worked long enough in the hospital during the war to know the addictive effects of such a concoction and also its potential hazards, but equally this was a medicine prescribed by a family doctor and all the ingredients were common enough in treatments. If Amelia had been on this medicine some time then it was difficult to say what complications sudden withdrawal might cause. Clara preferred not to risk killing the woman by doing nothing. She took the bottle to Amelia.

"Is this the blue stuff?" She asked.

Amelia looked physically exhausted now, she was trembling all over and sobbing, her hands still worked sporadically to try and scare off the birds or whatever other hallucinations she was experiencing. She managed to nod.

Clara made up a draught of the medicine in a glass using water from a jug sitting on the bedside table. She offered it with some reluctance to Amelia, but the woman grabbed for it and drank with relish. It took very little time before her body relaxed and she seemed to be enveloped in a sort of peace. Clara helped her to her bed – Amelia was in a stupor – then carefully hid the bottle back away in William Henry's shaving kit. She went to inform Miss Sampford of developments and to summon a doctor. It was only half past ten in the morning and already the house was in chaos yet again.

Chapter Twenty One

Dr Harrison arrived within half an hour – that was the advantage of living at a good London address and being known as a patient who paid her bills promptly, Miss Sampford explained candidly. Dr Harrison had been attending Miss Sampford for nearly twenty years and was on good enough terms with his oldest patient to feel comfortable addressing her by her Christian name as he entered the door.

"Dear Edith, whatever is the matter? Not like you to summon me to a house call?"

"It is not for me Dr Harrison," Miss Sampford hastily assured him, "But for my poor niece-in-law who has taken quite a funny turn. May I introduce Miss Clara Fitzgerald who is a friend staying with me this Christmas? She was present when Amelia became unwell."

"Miss Fitzgerald." Dr Harrison offered a hand to shake, "Might you explain what has occurred while we head to the patient?"

Clara outlined the strange behaviour of Amelia as they mounted the stairs, remarking that Elijah had said she had been talking to herself at night.

"We might at first assume this was a nervous breakdown caused by the suicide of her husband." Clara elaborated, "But the fact she had a bottle containing some sort of medicine, which she had clearly been taking for some time, indicates this is a long standing problem."

"It sounds like a case of acute hysteria." Dr Harrison nodded, "Has she ever been seen by a psychiatrist?"

"I doubt William Henry would ever allow such a thing." Miss Sampford answered as she followed the doctor and Clara upstairs.

"Shame. Some of them are really rather good."

Dr Harrison was directed into the patient's bedroom where she still lay prone on the bed, a dreamy, contented look on her face.

"Where is this medicine?" He asked.

Clara retrieved the bottle from its hiding place and handed it to the doctor.

"I realise its atrocious stuff, but the state she was in I didn't think it sensible to keep it from her."

Dr Harrison placed a pair of small glasses on his nose and peered at the label on the bottle.

"Hmm." He said to himself, "It is not for me to judge my fellow physicians, but this would knock out a horse. How long do you suppose she has been taking it?"

Clara had no answer for that. Dr Harrison went to the bed, took Amelia's pulse and listened to her heart. He snapped his fingers over her face to see if she responded, there was no movement.

"Aside from her late husband, does she have anyone to care for her?" He asked, looking sadly at Amelia.

"I'm afraid there is no one." Miss Sampford admitted, "Servants, of course."

"At the least she needs a nurse." Dr Harrison responded, "Someone who could monitor her emotional state and administer medicine. I would not be happy allowing a woman in such a state to self-medicate. But before that I would highly recommend she attend a private hospital where they can assess her mental and physical state. I dare say they will also want her off this stuff," He indicated the blue medicine bottle, "and onto a more fitting medicine, but that is not going to be an easy process and should not be attempted at home."

"I shall have to discuss that with my brother." Miss Sampford sighed, "Thank you for coming Dr Harrison."

"Not a problem, Miss Sampford."

Clara offered to see the doctor out, which afforded her an opportunity to speak with him in private.

"Doctor, may I ask, could Amelia be potentially dangerous?"

"In what way?" Dr Harrison looked at her curiously.

Clara decided to hedge around the truth.

"Matters have been strained since the death of William Henry and Amelia has been increasingly hostile to others in the house, mainly in her manner of speaking. I wondered if there was any risk to other members of the household, particularly should she learn she is to be sent to a hospital. Might she react violently?"

Dr Harrison paused at the door.

"With cases like this anything is possible, I'm afraid. Though, in the main, I find the person they are usually most dangerous to is themselves."

Clara thanked him and watched him leave, his highly polished shoes skidding a little on the icy path. She closed the door and considered what he had said. Supposing, just supposing, the woman who had attempted to kill Miss Sampford last night had nothing to do with the actual ghost, but was Amelia pretending to be her? It was possible, by all means. Clara could not imagine any sane or rational person acting in such a manner. There had been a certain frenzied madness about the figure who leaned over her with a knife last night. And who better than a guest in the house to let herself in and out? But was that too complicated? Two people masquerading as ghosts in the same house (because the first ghostly appearance had occurred before Amelia's arrival)? Clara felt the idea a little preposterous, but she could not shake from her mind the idea that Amelia might be insane enough to murder her husband's aunt.

Clara made her way into the drawing room to compose her thoughts. Hilda and Edward Sampford were sitting reading as if nothing had occurred over the last few days. Clara was beginning to find them annoying.

"What was all that commotion about, dear?" Hilda glanced up from a book about the horticultural needs of Dahlias.

"Amelia took a funny turn." Clara answered.

Hilda gave her husband a knowing look.

"I said as much, did I not Edward? I said that girl was not right."

"That you did." Edward said, not looking up from a volume on the Napoleonic wars.

"She has been unwell a while?" Clara asked.

"Since the day William Henry married her." Hilda had a way of looking over her glasses that put Clara in mind of a rather pompous teacher she had once had, "Of course, her family is of good breeding which is presumably why he picked her."

"That and the money." Edward interjected solemnly.

"Well yes, and that." Hilda conceded, "Still, they managed all right I suppose. Though it's no wonder they had no children."

"At least we won't have any madness running through the family line." Edward added, with a rather satisfied tone.

Clara was rather relieved that Miss Sampford appeared at that moment.

"What an awful nightmare." She tutted, "The doctor wants Amelia sent to a hospital."

"Sounds wise to me, Edith, what else can you do with her? Can't have you nursing her here." Edward finally looked up from his book.

"I know, but I feel so awful about it. Like I am sending her to a madhouse. I keep thinking about what William Henry would say."

"William Henry clearly couldn't cope with the woman anymore." Hilda declared, "And instead of facing up to his problems he abandoned them to us. Sit down won't you Edith? You look done in."

"I feel that way too." Miss Sampford sank onto a sofa, "I have half a mind to be done with New Year's and ask you all to go home and let me recuperate in peace."

Clara caught the glance Miss Sampford threw at her as she spoke and realised she had finally demurred to Clara's suggestion. Neither Hilda nor Edward noticed the look.

"Really, you mustn't fret Edith." Hilda patted her hand affectionately.

"Old girl, you've got to keep strong. Can't have you going downhill too." Edward put an arm, rather stiffly, about his older sister's shoulders.

Clara decided she was now an interloper in a family moment and left the room. She had other business to attend to anyway. She pulled the note Elijah had handed her from her pocket and read the names. Elijah had provided both home addresses and places of employment for the individuals listed. Clara decided it was worth seeing if any of them worked on Boxing Day. She fetched her coat and hat and set off into the snow.

~ ~ * ~ ~

Sebastian Grey had trained as a lawyer, but his heart was never in it. Each term at university was a slog that wore him down a little bit more, until his father abruptly died in his final year and Sebastian came into his inheritance far sooner than he had expected. Suddenly the endless days of courtrooms and panelled offices that Grey had once dreaded disappeared as if into a bad dream and he was free to live his life as he chose. With no siblings to worry him, and only an elderly uncle to answer to, he left the countryside of Hertfordshire and took a flat in London, from there he pursued a career in show business.

Sebastian Grey was not much of a performer, but he had an eye for talent and within a year of setting himself up as a theatrical agent he quickly had a respectable client list. A little judicious investment in London theatres and playhouses earned him the favour of managers and actors alike. In short, at the stately age of 23, Grey was doing well for himself and he knew it.

Clara found him – after an abortive trip to his office – in the second row of red velvet seats at Pickerson's Variety Theatre. The manager was holding auditions and a number of young ladies were huddled around the stage door and inside the lobby, smoking like chimneys and trying to keep warm in their flimsy stage clothes. Grey was representing some of his clients who were hoping to get a spot in Pickerson's latest theatrical undertaking. Clara slipped in unnoticed, because theatres are never very well-guarded unless a performance is going on, and she walked through the stage door brazenly under the nose of the doorman, who took one look and assumed she was there to audition. Clara didn't disabuse him of the idea and found her way, after a few wrong turns, into the auditorium.

She didn't know what Grey looked like, but there were only two men in the seats and one was shouting directions at a group of five girls on stage. The second was lounging back in his chair, smoking a black cigarillo. Clara, deciding that an agent was unlikely to be directing girls on stage, plucked for the smoking man as the likely Sebastian Grey. She slipped into the row and shuffled towards him.

"Sebastian Grey?"

"Who's asking, sweetheart?" Grey gave her a leer that was so lascivious Clara found herself thinking Elijah had been hopelessly wrong about the man's inclinations.

"Clara Fitzgerald. Sorry to bother you. Might I have a word?"

"Are you a singer or a dancer?" Grey cast his eyes over her, "Or a comedienne? I'm not looking to represent one of those."

"I'm not a performer Mr Grey. I am a private detective, working on behalf of the Sampford family."

Grey showed no concern, just puffed on his cigarillo.

"What has that got to do with me?"

"Perhaps nothing. You see, I am trying to learn more about William Henry Sampford. I believe you were a friend of his?"

"Nope." Grey said, his grin never leaving his face, "Hey, Derek, you going to get those girls dancing or what?"

The man, who had been trying to show the girls the way he wanted them to stand on the stage, turned to Grey and gave a hefty shrug. Then he motioned to someone in the wings and music began to play.

"You watch this, sweetheart, these girls are corkers." Grey said to Clara, again his eyes roved over her, "Reckon you might be all right up there too. Men like a bit of flesh on their dancing girls, a bit of wobble and ripple."

Clara couldn't decide whether to be offended or (in an age when so many fashion magazines insisted girls with curves were abnormal) flattered. All she could safely say was that she was feeling most uncomfortable. Things began to get worse as the music ramped up and the girls on stage, who had previously been moving around in rather mundane theatrical poses, started to strip off their clothes.

"Told you they are corkers." Grey smirked as flimsy skirts and blouses dropped to the floor. It was the first time in Clara's life that she had seen another adult woman naked. That uncomfortable feeling was getting worse.

"Mr Grey, you do recall Elijah Sampford who you were at university with, I suppose?"

"Yeah, him? Boring as dishwater, old Elijah."

"Well, William Henry was his uncle. On Christmas Eve he shot himself."

Grey's grin froze a little. His still eyes followed the girls on stage, but Clara sensed his mind was elsewhere.

"I am not here to cause you any problems Mr Grey. All I am trying to discover is why William Henry took his own life. It has been suggested to me that I should speak to some of his special friends, and you, I was led to believe, were one of them."

"You were led to believe wrong." Grey stubbed out his cigarillo in one of the little ashtrays theatres have attached to the back of their seats.

"Mr Grey, please, your name will not be shared with anyone, but I fear William Henry was being blackmailed and this led to him taking his own life. Surely you want the person who drove him to such lengths caught?"

Grey said nothing.

"I appreciate a man of your inclinations has to be extremely careful."

"Inclinations?" Grey glanced at her, "What inclinations would those be?"

"Oscar Wilde loved the theatre too." Clara said in answer.

Grey snorted.

"I don't know who you have been talking with, but you have the wrong end of the stick, love. I spend my days surrounded by beautiful, semi-clad women. What more do you need to know?"

"And I imagine not a single one of those girls ever goes home with you." Clara looked at him pointedly, "I am not judging Mr Grey, I just need help understanding William Henry. I thought you might give me some answers."

"You thought wrong, sweetheart." Grey's attention was back on his dancers, "Well Derek? I said they were beauts."

Derek gave him a shrug.

"Seen a dozen like them already."

Grey threw up his hands in frustration.

"Girls, get your clothes on before you catch your death and I'll talk some sense into our dear theatre manager." Grey rose from his seat, glancing at Clara as he did so, "Sorry I can't help. You should think about being a dancer, I could use a girl with your curves."

"No, thank you." Clara rose also, "I am very particular about remaining fully clothed."

Grey grinned at her.

"Can't win 'em all." He winked.

"No, you can't Mr Grey," Clara nodded at him as she left, "No you can't."

~ ~ * ~ ~

Clara's next stop was Mason's Bank, where she anticipated finding the young Mr Winston Mason – Boxing Day being no excuse in the banking world for not making money, after all. The bank, as she had expected, was open and a steady stream of customers were wandering in and out, apparently making up for the one day of the year (excluding Sundays) the bank had been shut. Clara wandered into a large foyer with towering Grecian pillars and faux marble-work everywhere. She paused for a moment to take in the decoration which screamed of expense and indulgence, then she headed for the nearest unengaged cashier.

"Hello, might I ask if Mr Winston Mason is in?"

The cashier looked a little surprise to be asked such a request then turned around to speak to someone behind him.

"Might I ask what it is about?" The cashier said on returning to his station.

"You can say I have come on behalf of Mr William Henry Sampford and that it is extremely important. My name is Clara Fitzgerald, by the way."

Still looking puzzled the cashier asked her to wait as he moved away to a telephone and made a call. It was not long before he returned.

"Mr Mason is extremely busy." He apologised.

"Please, try again and this time state that I am here on behalf of the late Mr William Henry Sampford."

Once more the cashier retreated to the telephone, when he returned this time he was utterly confused.

"Mr Mason asks I escort you to his office at once."

The cashier came around his desk and led Clara to a short corridor where there was an elevator. A uniformed porter nodded to them both as he opened the lift doors and took them up to the third floor. The elevator opened onto a plush hallway decorated with paintings of famous bankers and members of the Mason family. A formidable row of businessmen glowered down at Clara from the walls as she walked past. She doubted many women, aside from the odd secretary, ever wandered these corridors and she found herself smiling at the grim faces that scowled down at her from their canvases.

The cashier stopped outside a rather plain door, the only ornamentation a simple name plate. He knocked and when a voice called out for him to come in, he entered and escorted Clara inside.

"Miss Fitzgerald, sir." He announced, before disappearing as fast as he had arrived.

Clara took a pace into the room as the door clicked behind her. Winston Mason sat behind his desk, a slender young man with slicked back hair and a pencil moustache. He was not precisely handsome, his nose being rather on the prominent side, but he had lively, charming eyes that drew you in. He was wearing a pale grey suit and had his hands clutched before him on the desk.

"Miss Fitzgerald, please take a seat and explain what this is all about."

Clara sat in a chair facing the desk and composed herself to break what she suspected would be very bad news to the young banker.

"I'm sorry to call without an appointment." She began.

"No matter… you mentioned something about calling on behalf of Mr William Henry Sampford. He does not bank here, you realise?" Mr Mason was avoiding her eyes and speaking very carefully.

"I am not here on banking business, I am afraid. I wanted to speak to you personally, seeing as you were a friend of Mr Sampford."

"I barely know the man." Mason let out what might have been an attempt at a light-hearted laugh, "I have heard his name, of course. His aunt banks with us, a very loyal customer."

"I suppose that is how you met him? Perhaps he came to discuss his aunt's financial arrangements, though it would have been improper for you to have discussed them with him."

"I really don't know the man."

Clara paused and assessed Mason, he was hiding something from her, she knew it, but drawing him out would require a great deal of tact. She tried again.

"I'm sorry to hear that Mr Mason, I really came to you because I am clutching at some rather loose straws. On Christmas Eve William Henry Sampford apparently shot himself. I say apparently because I am still trying to work out why and also the event took place in a household where there has been some considerable trouble." Clara took a breath, "In Mr Sampford's possession was a large sum of money in a suitcase. Not the sort of thing someone brings with them when they visit an aunt at Christmas. This makes me wonder if his suicide was driven by blackmail, and if that is the case, I have to ask myself what was Mr Sampford being blackmailed about? Without boring you, Mr Mason, I am aware of William Henry's proclivities and I am led to believe you knew of them too. Now, it is only my personal opinion, but if a man kills himself because a person is blackmailing him I look upon that as murder as much as if they pulled the trigger themselves. But no one will talk to me! You are my last hope. You say you hardly knew him, but perhaps you know of some gentleman in London who could assist me? Something must explain William Henry's regular trips to the city. And if there is a blackmailer I fully intend to find them and do what little I can to see they are brought to some sort of justice."

Her speech concluded Clara fell silent and waited for Mason's response. The young banker stared at the blotter on his desk for some time, tapping one index finger on the very edge of it. When he raised his head his face was extremely pale.

"William Henry…" He swallowed hard, "This is unexpected."

Clara waited, the temptation to interject a question was strong, but she sense that this was a time to keep quiet. Mason turned his head and thought for a long time. His finger still tapped absently.

"William used to come down to London to see me." He spoke at last.

Clara realised she had been holding her breath and released it.

"You were good friends?" She asked gingerly.

"Very good friends." Mason was breathless with emotion, "You don't seem shocked, Miss Fitzgerald? I presume you understand my implication?"

"I understand it well enough." Clara said gently, "As for being shocked, well, I don't shock easily Mr Mason and certainly not because a man admits to me he is homosexual."

"Ah," Mason said, a little uncomfortable with hearing the word out loud, "How is Amelia coping with her loss?"

Clara sighed.

"I don't think 'coping' is the word to use." She said sadly, "She has had a mental breakdown."

"That doesn't surprise me." Mason replied, "William said she was a very disturbed person. He told me once he thought of himself and Amelia as two desperately lost souls that no one understood, and one day it occurred to him he might marry her and take care of her, and in return his father would no longer hound him about finding a wife. I think he also looked upon it as penance for his desires, she was his burden, his cross to bear for his sins, and he bore that burden gladly."

"I am not sure what will become of Amelia without him." Clara said, realising she at last was seeing a decent side to William Henry, "And what about you?"

Mason grimaced.

"What about me?" He said with a grim laugh, "He was just a friend, after all."

"Mr Mason, you may find my next offer in poor taste, but it is meant with only good intentions. If you wish at any time to talk about what you are feeling I will be a willing listener."

"You are very kind Miss Fitzgerald, but I must ask, what is your involvement in all this?" Mason was suddenly looking very suspicious, and Clara realised he probably assumed she was a reporter or something awful like that.

"I am a private detective, Mr Mason. I came to No.50 to investigate Miss Sampford's ghost issue. If I might take you into my confidence?"

"Go ahead, you already know enough about me. I can assure you I am good with secrets."

"The ghost of No.50 Berkeley Square is no more a spectre than you or I, but a very real, living person who has murderous designs on Miss Sampford. Now, it just so happens that the window the ghost has been using to enter and exit the property is in the very room William Henry died. I don't like coincidences Mr Mason and so I have found myself wondering about whether there was a connection between the two. And then I find the money and it strikes me as a pay-off to someone, but who? A blackmailer? An assassin William Henry has hired to bump off his aunt?"

"William Henry did not wish his aunt dead." Mason said sharply, his face tightening into a pained expression.

"I must admit, his death seems to imply that. But the money?"

"I can explain that too." Mason was so desperately trying to control himself that his words came out in a staccato stutter, "William Henry did not wish his aunt dead, but I would be lying to you if I said he did not find her continued residence in No.50 a nuisance on his bank account. He wanted to free up the money used to sustain her for his own estate, but he was not going to murder her over it!"

"Then how did he intend to free the money?"

Mason closed his eyes for a moment and then groaned.

"William had gone over every detail of his grandfather's financial arrangement for Miss Sampford. There was a clause within it that mentioned what would occur if Miss Sampford become incapable through physical or mental deterioration to continue to reside on her own. In such a situation, the money set aside for her allowance would instead be used to fund her future care. William saw this as a loophole; if he proved his aunt was incapable of continuing to live at No.50, he could insist on her coming to live at the Sampford estate so that he and Amelia might care for her. And then her allowance would be paid to them to maintain her."

Clara understood. It was a rather dastardly plan, but it wasn't murder.

"William would have taken good care of her." Mason added hastily.

Clara felt that was by-the-by.

"How did he intend to prove Miss Sampford was incapable?" She asked.

"He had heard the talk about the ghost at No.50. The stories are all over London and his nephew Elijah kept mentioning it. It seemed to him, that all he need do was convince people the ghost was a product of his aunt's mind, and then he would be able to prove she was unable to continue residing alone."

"He intended to demonstrate his aunt was senile?"

"Yes, but as I am sure you are aware she is clearly not, so to strengthen his case he set about finding a doctor who would testify that Miss Sampford was mentally incapable." Mason paused, "I suspect that is what the money you found was for. Paying off this doctor. On his last visit to me he said he had found someone willing to diagnose Miss Sampford with whatever he wanted."

"This is utterly disgraceful." Clara could hardly contain herself any longer, "Stripping a woman of her independence in such a way!"

"I know, I know. I didn't agree with it either, but what could I do? If I came forward it would mean explaining how I came to know William's plans."

"And it would also mean losing him." Clara calmed down, "Did he also manufacture the ghost?"

"No, that was pure luck. In any case, William thought that was a load of nonsense, or the servants misbehaving."

Clara found the whole thing ghastly, but it certainly made a good deal of sense. It explained his conversation with Amelia which Annie overheard. William had been intending to make the pay-off over Christmas. However that raised a new dilemma.

"Oh dear." She tutted to herself, "That makes it all the less likely he shot himself."

"William was never suicidal." Mason suddenly spoke with a spark of anger, "I know that is how everyone thinks us 'queers' meet our ends, a pistol to our heads or a bottle of Arsenic, but just because you live a double life doesn't mean you regard that life as any less precious. William had no reason to kill himself. He had me, and no one else knew that. He was safe and he was happy."

Clara smiled at Mason, knowing all too well that what a person projected on the outside by no means reflected what they were feeling on the inside. But she had to agree that William seemed to have far more reasons to want to live, than he had to want to die. His suicide had been bothering her since it occurred. It was not so much the lack of a note, though that was troubling, but the way he had been muttering to himself just before – and the pistol. No one seemed quite able to say where that had come from. It was the timing that also disturbed her. To stand up and leave in the middle of a card game to kill oneself seemed rather odd. Yet she could not offer any other reason for why he had left the room, nor how he had ended up in the empty spare room.

"If he didn't kill himself, then I am looking for a murderer." She said at last.

"This ghost? You said the person behind it was a killer."

"Maybe, but how did he end up in that room? I need to think this over further; there must be some logic to it." Clara impulsively reached out her hand and placed it over Mason's, "I appreciate you being so candid with me. I shall not repeat this meeting to anyone, of that I can assure you."

"Thank you, Miss Fitzgerald, for seeking me out. Had you not come I would not have known of William's death until I read about it in the newspapers, and that would have been far worse." Mason rose to show her out of his office.

"Will you be all right?" Clara asked with real concern.

"I don't suppose I have much option but to be all right." He answered morbidly. He hesitated at the door of his office, "I loved him, Miss Fitzgerald. One shouldn't say that about another man, but that is how it was."

"I understand Mr Mason, I really do. And I am sorry for your loss."

Mason gave her a faint smile and then escorted her to the elevator. There was no more talk of William Henry, which was how Clara had expected it to be. When they reached the lift Mason wished her well, as if she was just another of his banking clients. Clara stepped into the elevator feeling deeply sadden. Life could be very hard and cruel, she mused, and this business of being a private detective – delving into everyone's secrets – sometimes seemed a very unpleasant thing. If it wasn't for people in desperate need like Miss Sampford, Clara would dare say she would have given it up a long time ago.

Chapter Twenty Two

"There is a gentleman waiting for you in the dining room, madam." Humphry greeted Clara on the doorstep with his usual sombre expression, "He appears to be that fellow from the paper."

Clara thanked the butler and headed to the dining room where she found the newspaper reporter Hawkins sitting at a table and helping himself to a plate of mince pies.

"Ah, there you are!" He stood, brushing off crumbs from his shirt and offered his hand to shake.

"You have news, Mr Hawkins?"

"I do indeed, took a bit of digging but then I came up trumps."

"About William Henry?"

"No, nothing about him, well, there was stuff but it wasn't very exciting. I did chase a few of my contacts but your William Henry was a sly beggar and I came up empty-handed."

"Never mind him then, I presume you have some worthwhile information on Miss Sampford?" Clara took a seat at the dining table, her head ached and she couldn't decide if she was hot or freezing cold. Wandering about in the snow was doing nothing for her streaming nose and sore throat.

"Now, Miss Sampford gave me quite a surprise." Hawkins resumed his own seat, "Mince pie? You don't look well."

"I have a winter cold." Clara explained, taking a mince pie and nibbling at the corner. It was warm and straight from the oven, "And this case is wearisome."

"I know how it is, flog yourself silly trying to trace down loose ends and come up with the best story and at the end of the day you wonder if it was all worth it. I'm still not sure why I keep at it, something in the blood I reckon. I can't let a good story go." Hawkins grinned, "Talking of stories, did you see the piece in the paper this morning?"

"I missed it." Clara confessed.

"I came prepared for that." Hawkins opened a leather bound notebook and removed a newspaper clipping. He slipped it across the table to Clara.

The top of the page was dominated by a picture of Berkeley Square taken at a wide angle, just beneath this image a large headline read "Berkeley Square Ghost: Truth or Fiction?" Under that was a long article going over the details of the haunting and the interview with Miss Sampford. Care had been taken to not specify the house number, nor reproduce Miss Sampford's real name. Not that anyone who had spent any time in London recently would be fooled about which house it was referring to. Clara read the piece carefully.

"A very balanced article." She said at last, "Was your editor pleased?"

"Delighted! The Boxing Day paper is the worst to fill and not always easy to sell, but this story has had it jumping off the shelves."

"Good." Clara pushed the clipping back towards him, "But what about Miss Sampford?"

Hawkins held up a finger, indicating she should wait, and then opened his notebook. He flicked through a few pages of shorthand that looked to Clara like no written language on earth and then came to a halt.

"Here it is. I couldn't trawl through every single issue over the span of Miss Sampford's lifetime looking for her name – it would have taken weeks – so I concentrated on her time with the Suffragettes, my theory being that was the most likely period when anything significant might have happened."

"Reasonable." Clara concurred with him.

"Going through the papers, one story jumped out at me and I remembered seeing some unpublished notes. You see, not everything a reporter collects can be published, but sometimes the editor sees fit to keep the reporter's notes for future reference. That was when I remembered seeing Miss Sampford's name before. I went to the files where notes on stories are archived and did a quick name search, and there she was!

"In a story your editor could not publish?"

"Exactly, only it was a different editor back then, but the same principle. Anyway, I pulled out the file and compared it with the stories I had found in the papers, and it all seemed to add up. Of course, it was all circumstantial, not enough to stick your neck out and publish names and so forth, but I reckon you will find it interesting."

"You are keeping me in dreadful suspense Mr Hawkins." Clara informed him with a slight chastising tone, "Are you going to explain what you found?"

"Right, yes, sorry I ramble when I get the whiff of a good story."

"I fully understand, but what is that story?"

Hawkins pulled his notes in front of him and pressed a finger firmly beneath the start of his shorthand scrawl on the topic of Miss Sampford.

"I found the story in one of the October issues from 1913. As I am sure a lady of your political acumen is aware, that was the year the suffrage movement was really hotting up and I mean really!" Hawkins was getting excited again, "We had paintings being slashed in the

National Gallery, houses being set on fire and threats of bombs, it was all so sensational!"

"And did the good cause the ladies were attempting to promote no favours whatsoever." Clara sighed, "Things had gone too far."

"In any case, that sets the scene for the events I am about to describe." Hawkins tapped his notes, "On 12 October 1913 six ladies set off from the Christchurch home of Mrs Allens, who happens to be one of the heads of the 'Women for Reform Movement'. Mrs Allens, herself, was not with them, but the police strongly believed she had given them instructions for the evening. In any case, these six suffragettes were carrying between them a basket of old lemonade bottles that they had filled with oil or some sort of fuel, to make fire bombs."

"Oh good lord!" Clara shuddered at the thought.

"What we know for certain is that on that same night six houses belonging to MPs known to be antagonistic to the suffragette cause were set on fire using such devices. The ladies who threw the bombs were never officially identified, though in the notes I uncovered was included a list of names from an unknown source."

"I have a nasty feeling you are about to tell me Miss Sampford was on that list."

Hawkins gave an apologetic smile.

"Six houses went up in flames, all bar one were empty at the time. The home of Mr Sidney Edgbarton was supposed to have been empty that night, Edgbarton being away in the country. But the MP's daughter, 14-year-old Christina, had become ill with scarlet fever and the whole family had returned to their London home late that evening. The suffragettes had clearly not been informed of this change in the Edgbartons' plans; had they been I suspect they would have called off the attack on Edgbarton's house."

"We have to hope." Clara agreed.

"Around nine o'clock the household had mostly gone to bed. The daughter was confined to her bed upstairs with a nursemaid to hand. Mrs Edgebarton came downstairs for some reason and went into the front drawing room carrying a candle. Her husband joined her. With the drapes closed and only a candle for light it would have been impossible to know from the outside that anyone was indoors."

"And yet they were."

"Yes, it was just after nine – the nursemaid said about a quarter past the hour – when she heard a terrific smash followed by dreadful screams and shouts. She ran down the main stairs and to her horror saw smoke coming from beneath the door of the drawing room. She ran towards it and reached out for the brass door knob which was already red hot and burned her hand. She started to shout for help and more servants appeared. The drawing room was completely engulfed in fire by this time. There was no sign of Mr or Mrs Edgbarton. Christina was hastily carried out and deposited in a neighbour's house while the fire brigade was called. As you may imagine there was panic among the neighbourhood, lest the whole street be set ablaze. Fortunately the fire brigade arrived promptly and the fire was brought under control within the hour. It was only when the chaos had calmed down did anyone set foot in the drawing room.

"There they found the bodies of the unfortunate Mr and Mrs Edgbarton, burned almost beyond recognition, but she was still wearing a diamond necklace that had survived the flames and he was identifiable by his unique dentistry work. The remnants of the fire bomb were found too. After studying the scene the fire brigade concluded that the bottle had smashed the window and struck Mrs Edgbarton, setting her alight. As she stumbled about, setting the room ablaze, her husband tried to come to her aid. He was either set on fire trying to help his wife, or died in the smoke. The room was engulfed in fire within minutes and there would have been no possibility of escape."

Clara closed her eyes and tried not to linger too long on the image of Mr and Mrs Edgbarton burning alive.

"What of the culprit?" She asked with trepidation.

"Neighbours reported seeing an older woman running away after the smash and the scream. The woman had grey hair that was uncovered. Having gone through the list of suspects I found among notes on the story, there is only one likely culprit."

"I knew you were going to say that." Clara sighed, "Miss Sampford."

"Yes. Naturally there was public outcry over the incident. When Miss Edgbarton had recovered from scarlet fever she made a very emotive appeal in the papers for someone to come forward with information. I suspect the police had a list similar to the one I found in our archives, but without evidence they could do little about it. The only people who could provide the testimony they would need for a conviction were the very women behind the attack. Coming forward would mean implicating themselves and none would do that. Besides, it was a matter of principle. Emmeline Pankhurst released a pamphlet attacking the police for always blaming suffragettes for these actions and then ruined her argument by using the fires as an example of the passionate feelings running through the suffrage cause."

"Oh dear." Clara said to herself, "Was anyone brought to justice?"

"No. The matter continued to cause outrage until the ugly beast of war raised its head and Germany took everyone's attention."

"And what of Christina?"

"I can't say. Was this the sort of story you were looking for?"

"Well, it would make me want to kill someone." Clara declared.

"Then... what now?"

Clara rested her chin in her hand, bracing her elbow on the table. She had a lot to mull over, but first there were important matters to be dealt with. Hawkins waited patiently until Clara's attention came back to him.

"You wanted a scoop Mr Hawkins and you have kept your side of the agreement. I suggest you remain here tonight, I suspect there will be a story in it if you do."

"Might Miss Sampford object?"

"I'll hide you in Tommy's room. Tonight everything will happen and then we will know who is behind the ghost of Berkeley Square."

Hawkins gave her a huge grin and bundled up his shorthand into one pile.

"The editor will be delighted."

"Just remember you are dealing with peoples' lives and I expect tact."

"Miss Fitzgerald, tact is my middle name." Hawkins assured her.

"If that is the case, I suspect you to be quite unique in the world of journalism." Clara grimaced, wondering that she had done, "I do hope Miss Sampford can forgive me."

Chapter Twenty Three

It was close to midnight by the time Clara had her party ready for action. She hoped the rumours of Miss Sampford sending home her guests would be enough to smoke out the ghost, the rest of her plan was simple enough; once the ghost was in the house she wasn't getting out again. Presuming the ghost's accomplice would leave a door unlocked for her, Clara issued all her team with keys and instructions on how she was going to cordon off the second floor. Andrews and Captain Adams were roped in after Clara explained the situation to them. The knowledge that Simon Jones had been killed by a very living person had had the effect of even quietening Andrews' objections, though he still maintained the idea that this was really a savage Elemental. Adams and Andrews were stationed secretly on the second floor landing, the idea was that when the ghost appeared and entered the second floor corridor (depending on whether she came down the main stairs or via the back stairs) they would quietly follow and block her exit. Clara stationed Oliver on the first floor landing of the back stairs. He was to creep up and block the back stairs door with a chair, as soon as he was confident the ghost was in the corridor.

Meanwhile Tommy was stationed downstairs with the key for the front door. He was to keep watch from the dining room and note who unlocked the door in the entrance hall. Once it was safe he was to lock the door again and then place himself at the foot of the stairs to block an escape. Clara and Annie had the most difficult and dangerous task of all. They were to remain in Miss Sampford's bedroom and surprise the ghost when she entered. Clara was determined that at all costs she would protect Miss Sampford and trap her assassin. As soon as she raised the alarm all the men were to run to assist her, as long as they had completed their own tasks.

The idea that Annie and Clara would be confronting an armed, and possibly insane, woman on their own had not gone down well. Oliver had even suggested calling in Elijah as a third party to help the girls. But Clara refused. She had to keep her party to those who were least likely to have a motive to harm Miss Sampford, she could not rule out Elijah, nor the other members of the Sampford family. Equally Miss Sampford was appalled at the idea of having men in her room while she was in her night clothes. There was nothing for it, Clara insisted, but to leave the ambush to her and Annie. Tommy had scowled about this. Annie was not exactly delighted either, but she understood the logic. The only thing that finally placated matters was Captain Adams handing Clara an old army pistol he had brought with him as back-up should the shotgun fail. Clara accepted it graciously, knowing full well she had no intention of using it.

When everyone had gone to bed Clara's ambush party quietly arranged themselves into position. The house was silent and care was taken not to disturb those outside of the plan, even Humphry and the servants had been excluded from the mission. Clara was taking no chances.

Accompanied by a downcast Annie, she went to Miss Sampford's room. Miss Sampford was in bed, the covers pulled up to her chin, looking as frightened as a rabbit that has just heard the bay of hounds.

"Is that you Clara?" She hissed into the darkness.

"Yes." Clara replied as she carefully locked the door. Everything had to appear normal to avoid arousing suspicion, "Don't fret Miss Sampford, this will all be over soon."

"So you say, my dear, so you say." Miss Sampford's words were muffled by the blankets.

Annie gave the fire a good jab with the poker – the room was icy cold – and then sat down in a chair. Clara followed her example and sat too. They were in complete darkness except for the glow of the fire and the temptation to fall asleep was ever present. Annie gave Clara a nudge with her foot.

"You are sure this is a person?"

"Yes Annie, a living, breathing person."

Annie was silent for a moment.

"I'm not sure if that makes me more nervous or less."

"Go for less, we don't need nerves tonight."

The two women sat in silence. After a while the heavy sounds of breathing coming from the bed indicated that, despite her fears, Miss Sampford had fallen asleep. Clara envied her. Her cold was in its worst stage yet; she was constantly reaching for a hanky and feeling hot and light-headed. All she wanted was to climb into bed and sleep for as long as possible, but that would simply not do. She glanced over at Annie and could just see the glimmer of the girl's eyes.

"Annie, if I fall asleep you have to kick me."

"I like the way you think I won't fall asleep."

"Do you suppose Oliver will stay awake?"

Annie mulled this over.

"I think that very unlikely."

"That's what I fear."

The minutes ticked by. Clara found herself growing to dislike clocks more and more, there was something very dogmatic and militaristic about the way they crisply marked time. Her eyes started to close. A sharp pain in her ankle roused her.

"Ow. How did you know?"

"I was falling asleep, so I figured you must be too." Annie's voice was jovial despite their late-night mission.

"What time do you suppose it is? I can't remember hearing the clock chime."

"Shush! What was that?"

Both women paused and listened. In the corridor someone stepped very stealthily along the carpet runner, only the faintest creak coming from the floorboards. Clara held her breath. The footsteps drew closer ever so slowly. They were coming from the direction of the back stairs. She desperately hoped Oliver had remained awake and spotted the 'ghost'. She rose very carefully and walked quickly to the far side of the room, positioning herself to one side of the door so she could block any escape attempt. Annie also stood and damped down the fire so there was no light at all in the room, and then she slipped to the window and hid behind the drapes, ready to spring out at a moment's notice.

The footsteps drew to the door and a key slid into the lock. It was turned slowly, making as little noise as possible. Clara flattened herself against the wall and wondered why she had come up with this crazy plan in the first place, if anything happened to either Miss Sampford or Annie she would never forgive herself.

The door handle creaked and the door swung open. A veiled woman crept inside and pushed the door shut behind her. The room was so dark she had to reach out a hand to find the bedpost, then she lifted her veil so she could see what she was doing. Clara was behind her, watching her hands. The veil lifted, the ghost woman reached to her belt and pulled out a knife. Its sharp blade seemed to cut through the darkness as she raised it up in both hands.

Clara sprang. She grabbed the woman about the waist and dragged her off her feet and to the floor. Annie jumped from behind the curtain as the woman attempted to swing round the blade and stab Clara. Annie grabbed at the knife arm. The ghost woman screeched and flailed her other arm at Annie, snatching at her skirt and then her ankle, trying to pull her down too. Clara was half under her on the floor, but managed to reach up and wrap her fingers around the woman's wrist, holding tight to the arm that wielded the knife. Then Clara started to shout.

The next few moments flew by in confusion. The woman bit Annie's leg and Annie kicked her (muttering an apology as she did so). Clara wrenched at the knife arm and tried to lever the woman's fingers from the hilt of the blade. The woman flailed her legs furiously, writhing on the floor like a snake and almost throwing herself out of the grasp of both women. Miss Sampford sat up in bed and started to scream, and scream, and scream.

The bedroom door flew open and the lights flashed on. Oliver was jumping into the fray, sitting on the woman and wrestling her for the knife. Captain Adams and Andrews were not far behind, nor were the rest of the household, now roused by Miss Sampford's screams. The struggle lasted only seconds more. The woman's desperate strength finally left her and the knife dropped from her fingers and clattered to the floor. Clara pulled the woman's arms behind her and tied them with a cord Annie quickly handed her. Only later did she learn Annie had swiped it earlier in the night from Mr Humphry's dressing gown. There were a few more moments of furious struggling, then the woman gave in. She hung her head, panting hard, finally subdued. Someone turned on the electric light and Miss Sampford gazed into the face of her would-be killer. She was disappointed not to recognise it.

Clara, feeling rather ill and dizzy, got to her feet and stood over the Berkeley Square ghost. She was rather breathless and it was a second before she could say;

"Good evening, Christina Edgbarton."

The ghost looked up. She had a very pretty and very young face that was wrought with hatred. She glowered at Clara and then Miss Sampford. In her bed Miss

Sampford had heard the name and gone very pale. Clara needed no further proof that Hawkin's assumptions had been correct.

"It's time we called the police." She instructed the room, "Then might I ask everyone to come down to the dining room? I think a strong cup of tea and an explanation are in order."

Clara had Christina escorted to the library and sat her down in a chair. Oliver waited outside while Clara questioned the Berkeley Square ghost alone. Christina sat hunched, her head down, her lips set in a line of resignation and resentment. Clara sensed this was not going to be an easy conversation.

"I know all about your parents Christina." She began, "I know that is why you have come after Miss Sampford."

Christina's head shot up. She gave Clara a vicious scowl.

"But you won't let me kill her!"

"No." Clara said firmly, "Another death will not make things better. You would end up facing the noose and I hardly think your parents would want that."

"How would you know?" Christina snarled, "All I wanted was for some sort of justice. The police couldn't offer me it, so I had to take matters into my own hands."

"Your actions are still illegal."

"But justified!"

"And what of Simon Jones? What had he done to you?"

Christina looked blank.

"Who?"

"The man you pushed down the stairs the other night when he chased you." Clara explained patiently.

"Oh him." Christina gave a slight shrug, "He shouldn't have pursued me. I couldn't have him revealing me as the ghost before I was done. I didn't mean to kill him. I just shoved him away."

"And yet because of you he is dead." Clara sighed sadly, "What about William Henry? Why did he have to die?"

"William Henry? William Henry Sampford?" Christina looked puzzled, then she let out a sharp laugh, "I didn't kill him! I heard he shot himself. I stayed away from the house that night."

"But he died in the room you used to enter this house." Clara insisted.

"What does that prove? I never shot him, for that matter I don't have a pistol." Christina smirked, "Not such a clever detective, are you?"

"I wouldn't look so smug if I was you." Clara was annoyed, "After all, you walked into my trap. I suppose your accomplice failed to warn you?"

"Accomplice? What accomplice?" Christina's eyes flicked away as she spoke and this time Clara was sure she was lying.

"You need say no more, the police will arrive shortly and there are more than enough witnesses to testify to how you attacked Miss Sampford."

Christina snorted.

"She deserved it! The old cow. She ruined my life!" Christina growled, "Why are you protecting her?"

"Only because two wrongs don't make a right. I understand how you are feeling Christina, I would probably feel the same..."

"Don't try and sympathise with me!" Christina snarled, "Go fetch the police, go! I want no more to do with you!"

With that Christina forcible shoved round her chair and faced the wall. Clara recognised a lost cause when she saw one. She quietly left the room, locked the door, and went downstairs to join the others.

The entire household was in the dining room looking sombre and tired. Humphry was serving tea or coffee, depending on preferences, while Mrs James and the maids were sitting in the corner yawning. Clara came to the head of the table and rested her hands on the back of a chair. She felt exhausted and ill, yet there was still much more to be done.

"Upstairs in the library the ghost that has been troubling this house is safely secured." She began, her eyes wandering to Miss Sampford, "Her name is Christina Edgbarton, a very disturbed young woman who has been perpetrating this crime against Miss Sampford."

"But, why?" Edward Sampford looked up sharply from his coffee, "Why would anyone want to harm my sister?"

Clara's eyes had not strayed from Miss Sampford. The old woman now looked up at her pleadingly. Clara knew it was not her place to speak the truth, not yet at least.

"Miss Edgbarton holds a grudge against the suffragettes, who she blames for the deaths of her parents. She fixated on Miss Sampford as a former suffragette. As I said before, she is quite disturbed."

"But how did she get in?" Edward persisted, "She didn't walk through the walls like a ghost, now did she?"

"Miss Edgbarton used the renovation works next door at No.49 to aid her entry. As I discovered the other day, both houses have the same internal locks and keys, a cost-cutting measure by the original builders, no doubt. Christina stole a key from No.49, then made her way along the ledge of the third floor to one of the empty bedrooms. She pried up the window and slipped inside, before using the key from No.49 to unlock the bedroom door. She was then free to explore the house."

"But how did she know to enter that room?" Edward was getting demanding, his face had reddened. Clara realised he had surmised the same solution she had; Christina had an accomplice, someone who could tell her which room to enter, who could make sure the window was easy to open and who could test the keys from No.49 to make sure they worked.

"Miss Edgbarton wasn't working alone." Clara said, "Someone around this table was her accomplice and they are just as responsible for the death of Simon Jones and the near death of myself and Miss Sampford, as the woman upstairs."

A hushed silence fell on the room. Hilda Sampford glanced at the servants, but everyone else kept their eyes firmly on the table before them. Clara wanted to shake them all.

"I don't expect the accomplice to raise his or her hand, which is why I arranged for them to be caught in the act."

"What do you mean?" Elijah stuttered, his eyes bleary behind his round glasses.

"I was confident the accomplice would provide our ghost with a safe escape route, as they had done the night before. That night I found the front door unlocked, yet Humphry was always very careful about locking it. I suspected the accomplice had unlocked it in case Miss Edgbarton had to make a quick getaway. With so many people in the house, and after the fright caused by Simon Jones chasing her, a safe exit that didn't involve a scary climb along the brickwork was essential. Tonight I left one of my team downstairs to watch the hall and discover the accomplice." Clara paused, wanting to see if anyone confessed before she revealed what she knew. No one said anything, "Tommy, would you mind telling us who you saw unlock the front door?"

Tommy was sat to one side of the table in his wheelchair. He raised his head and looked along the row of anxious faces assembled around the dining table. Miss Sampford was perceptibly shaking in suspense.

"Tonight, I was hiding in this room. I had a clear view to the front door and just before midnight I saw Elijah walk down the stairs and unlock it."

Elijah gave a start.

"Nonsense!" He laughed, "You must have fallen asleep and dreamt it, old man."

"I didn't Elijah, and I have an extra witness to prove it." Tommy nodded to the door of the room. Clara walked around the table to the door and opened it to reveal Hawkins standing poised with his notebook.

"It was you all right Mr Sampford." Hawkins grinned at the assembled guests, "Saw it myself."

"What is that dreadful man doing here?" Hilda almost jumped from the table in disbelief.

"That is not important." Clara told her sternly, "What is, however, is why Elijah would help a woman murder his aunt."

"Elijah?" Miss Sampford asked tremulously, her whole body was shaking with emotion, "What have I done Elijah, to make you hate me so?"

"Nothing." Elijah said quietly, "I didn't expect her to go this far, that's all."

He raised his head and tried to catch the gaze of Hilda and Edward, but they avoided him. Instead he turned to Clara.

"I met her at a dance." He said, "She knew my name. She sought me out. I was in love with her before I knew it. Then she told me about her parents, about what had happened to them," He curled his lip in anger, "I didn't want to believe it, but she was so persuasive. She wanted revenge and somehow I found myself agreeing to it. I only thought she was going to scare my aunt. When I realised she had a knife, well…"

"But Elijah, you kept helping her long after you must have realised her murderous intentions?" Clara pointed out.

"I know! I just… couldn't stop. She said she would kill herself if I didn't help her. I… I couldn't let her do that and I would agree to anything… I would have stopped her from killing you, honestly auntie, I was all prepared. It was why I called in Andrews, I thought his presence and the other ghost hunters would stop her and then I would be back home and she would not be able to get into No.50 so easily."

"You called in Andrews to cover yourself." Clara said coldly, "It made it seem that you believed in the ghost."

"No!" Elijah shook his head, "I honestly wanted her stopped!"

"Simon Jones is dead because of you!" Andrews suddenly jumped from his seat and thrust an accusing finger at Elijah, "You led us into a trap! You tricked us!"

"No! No! It was not meant to be like this!" Elijah swore.

"I'll wring your neck!" Andrews yelled. Captain Adams leapt up to prevent him from flying across the table at Elijah, "How many more of us were you prepared to let die?"

"It got out of hand. I'm so sorry. I'm so sorry." Elijah dropped his head into his hands, his shame and guilt tumbling down upon him, "If I could make it right, I would, I swear."

"Elijah," Clara said coldly, "You continued to help a murderess long after you realised she was going to kill your aunt. You saw the knife she carried. If you were so intent on protecting your aunt, where were you tonight?"

Elijah shook his head sadly.

"I don't know why I didn't stop her." He admitted softly, "I told myself it was because I loved her, because I felt sorry for her. I felt she was justified in some way. But ultimately, I think I was too much of a coward to intervene and risk losing her. I love her so much."

"You... You... Murderer!" Andrews flung himself at Elijah again and had to be restrained.

"Leave him to the police." Captain Adams hissed at Andrews, wrestling him back to his chair, "The little toe-rag doesn't deserve to see you so upset."

"I hope they hang him!" Andrews snapped.

Clara let the room settle into an uneasy, but dangerous, silence before she raised the next topic liable to cause outrage.

"This family is rather good at keeping secrets." She said softly, "It's quite a talent you all have. I've resolved to my own satisfaction two of those secrets, but there is a third which I haven't unravelled. Who killed William Henry?"

"He shot himself." Edward Sampford said a little too quickly for Clara's liking.

"A number of things have suggested to me that was not the case. William Henry was on the verge of getting the very thing he had always wanted. Miss Sampford's money. This will be painful for you to hear Miss Sampford, but I must explain why I don't think William Henry killed himself." Clara gave a gentle smile to the old woman. It was not returned, "William Henry learned of the rumours of ghosts at this house and intended to use that gossip as evidence that Miss Sampford was losing her mind. He brought with him to London a large suitcase of money, which he intended giving to a pair of corrupt doctors to certify his aunt as insane. He would then insist that his aunt be placed in his care and her allowance turned over to him."

"I can't believe it!" Edward slammed a fist on the table, but Miss Sampford only looked miserable.

"I can." She said, "Go on Clara."

"That is the first reason I suspect William Henry was not a man on the verge of suicide. Next was the strange fact that he killed himself in an empty room. If he intended to commit suicide why go to the bother of using a different room from his bedroom? For that matter, why get up in the middle of a card game to do it? That was when another thought came to me. I had assumed when I heard William Henry's gruff responses he was talking to me, but what if he wasn't? What if there was another person in that room, someone speaking so softly that I could not hear them because I was standing outside the wrong door? When I heard the shot, found the room empty and raced for help, that person could have slipped out."

"And who would this person be?" Hilda Sampford asked very calmly.

"The list of possibilities is actually quite small. You see almost everyone was at the séance where I was present and first heard the footsteps of William Henry above.

That, after all, was why I went upstairs. Meanwhile I had Tommy downstairs to give an alibi to Elijah and Oliver. That left only three people who were alone in the drawing room. Hilda and Edward Sampford and Amelia Sampford."

"It's a lie!" Amelia rose from her seat and wailed at the room like a screaming banshee, "You can't say that! I never meant to kill him!"

"Sit down! Sit down!" Edward tried to pull the distraught woman back into her place, but she resisted him.

"I didn't even know he had brought the pistol until I was looking for my medicine." Amelia began to sob, "I only wanted to... to... to stop the voices. William wouldn't let me have more medicine, but I needed it."

"Do be quiet!" Edward snarled, "You are making it worse!"

"Edward, dear," Miss Sampford's voice cut through the confusion like ice, "Let her speak. I, for one, want to know what happened to my nephew."

Edward hesitated, but the stern gaze of his sister weakened his resolve. He let go of Amelia's arm and she ran around the table until she was near the fireplace, facing them all. Her hands shot to her mouth, she gabbled something to her fingers, then she flung out her arms and with a mad grimace announced;

"I killed him! I did it!"

"What did you do Amelia?" Clara asked in a light tone, her eyes flicking to Oliver and Tommy. Oliver slipped to the window nearest Amelia, while Tommy quietly wheeled himself around to the door where Hawkins stood. Amelia didn't pay them any heed.

"I only wanted my medicine and when I was searching for it, I found the gun. I couldn't find the little bottle and I was so... so... so tired." Amelia raked her fingers painfully through her hair, "The voices talk all the time, so many voices, and then they send the birds. The little birds that peck, peck, peck! I couldn't stand it anymore!

And there was this beautiful little pistol, all shiny in my hand and I said to the voices, I will show you!"

Amelia gave a strange laugh.

"I went into the spare room because I didn't want blood over all my pretty things and William would want to sleep in the bed later and he couldn't if I was all dead over it." Amelia gave a corpse-like grin, "I figured out ages ago that the doors all open by the same key. So I went into the empty room and I was all ready to do it. I had sat on the rug and had the gun at my temple when I realised I hadn't written a note, and I had to write a note so people would know I had only done it to defeat the voices. So I got up to get some paper and that's when I bumped into William heading to our room for a bottle of whisky he had brought with us. He saw the gun in my hand and I think he guessed what I was going to do. I ran back into the empty room and he followed me. I don't remember the next part clearly. I think I locked the door, because I had this idea we could die together and never be apart. But William insisting on having the gun and when I wouldn't give it to him he tried to grab it and we wrestled with it and then it just went... pop." Amelia gave a wail, biting her fingers, "I didn't mean to kill him. When he fell to the floor I dropped the gun. I had to tell someone, so we could get help for him. Doctors can fix all sorts of things these days. I ran out the room and down the back stairs because there was that stupid séance going on, and I didn't want any of them helping me. I didn't even realise there was someone in our bedroom. I ran to the drawing room and I told Hilda and Edward what had happened, and they made me sit down and do nothing, and say nothing."

Amelia took a shaky breath.

"How is William?" She glanced at Hilda.

Clara was very relieved that the police chose that moment to arrive at the door.

They were ushered inside and a doctor called for Amelia. The next few hours looked liable to be an endless barrage of questions.

Hawkins stood in the hall making rapid notes, he grinned at Clara.

"A scoop you said!" He laughed, "You don't half keep your promises miss!"

"Clara?"

Clara turned and saw Miss Sampford rising with difficulty from her chair.

"Clara, I would like to speak with you." The old woman grimaced with pain, then she tottered and had to cling to the side of the table.

Clara ran to her.

"The doctor is coming." She caught the woman as she fell, "Just hang on."

"I'm so sorry Clara." Miss Sampford gasped painfully, "I left... in my bedroom..."

Her fingers gripped fiercely to Clara's arm even as her eyes closed. Clara tried to pull her upright, but only succeeded in tumbling down to the floor with her.

"Miss Sampford!" She cried.

The old woman slumped in her arms.

"Miss Sampford?"

Humphry came running over and tried to help. Clara had tears running down her face as he lifted the woman from her. Brighton's first female private detective didn't need a doctor to tell her that Miss Sampford had stopped breathing.

Chapter Twenty Four

No.50 stood empty. The guests were all gone; Elijah had escaped the clutches of the police for the moment due to the influence of his family. He had returned home in shame, bitterly regretting his betrayal of his aunt. Edward and Hilda Sampford had equally been allowed to return home. They had insisted to the last that when Amelia told them she had killed her husband they did not believe her, and when William Henry was found with the pistol, they assumed the poor girl had confused his suicide for murder. Clara was unconvinced, but the police seemed to accept the story – after all, it was pretty obvious Amelia was insane. If she ever made it to trial they would be lucky, first the doctors would have to sedate her and attempt to restore some portion of her mind, if that was even possible. Edward had masked his brother's murder, from what Clara could gather, to avoid further family scandal. A suicide could be hushed up, but the murder trial of William Henry's insane wife could not. Besides, it was liable to bring out a lot of speculation and rumours that were not healthy for the Sampfords. In short, he would rather hide a murderer than risk the family name.

Clara had paid one further visit to Winston Mason to explain what she had discovered. She felt he deserved to learn of it from her rather than in a newspaper report. He took it quite calmly, but she suspected he was extremely practiced at hiding his emotions. All he could do when she was finished was nod.

"I thought he might have been killed because he cared for me." He said very quietly, "I thought maybe someone found out."

"No." Clara assured him, "The Sampfords are extremely good at keeping secrets."

The various surviving members of Andrews' ghost hunting party disappeared the day after the capture of Christina Edgbarton. Andrews was bitter and still cast dangerous glances at Elijah when he got the chance. Clara wondered if he would continue the hunt for the supernatural. She was saddened that his relatively harmless hobby had led to such tragedy, only wishing he had been prepared to listen to her sooner.

As for the servants, Jane and Flo packed their things and went to the nearest job exchange to find a new position. Mrs James declared she was going to her sister's house in Kent and had not thought much beyond New Year's. Mr Humphry muttered something about retirement and retreated to a friend's flat by the Thames. The house was left empty, except for Mr Mollinson, who came to inspect the premises and offered the Sampfords a hefty sum for it. They agreed to sell as soon as all the legal matters were sorted, of course. As far as Clara knew Miss Sampford's home was destined to soon become part of Mollinson's grand hotel.

Clara paid one last call on the house the morning before her train left for Brighton. She had left behind a silver bracelet in the confused haste to leave after Miss Sampford's death. She borrowed a key from Miss Sampford's solicitor and let herself in. Nothing had been removed yet and the house still had the same atmosphere as when Miss Sampford was alive. Clara stood in the hall and felt that at any moment the dear old lady would walk down the stairs. She was still struggling to resolve in her mind that this was the same woman who had burned to death two unfortunate souls. There were times in the dead of night when she went over the case and could understand Christina Edgbarton's point of view all too vividly. The girl was going to hang for the murder of Simon Jones, it was all the talk of the papers, but very little mention was made of the tragedy of her parents.

Clara climbed the stairs and went to her room. She pulled open a drawer and there was the bracelet. She slipped it around her wrist so she would not lose it again and felt its cold metal against her skin. Outside the door she heard someone walking.

Clara thought she was alone in the house. She went to the door and peered outside. There was no one present. Too many nights in No.50 had left her jumpy, Clara concluded. She made sure the house key was in her pocket and went to head downstairs. That was when she head distinct movement in Miss Sampford's old bedroom. It sounded like a drawer being opened.

Clara was now convinced there was an intruder, perhaps rummaging for money and valuables. She turned around and walked as swiftly as she could down the hall without making a noise. The sound of drawers being opened was still clear. Clara was going to give this burglar a piece of her mind, how dare they waltz into someone's home like this? Clara's hands balled into fists. She was suddenly very, very angry. Whoever was in Miss Sampford's bedroom was going to discover that Clara Fitzgerald could be very bad tempered.

She grabbed the door handle and rushed into the room, ready to jump on the intruder. She was rather disconcerted when she realised the room was empty. This had all too familiar echoes of William Henry. She was about to hasten out of the room, thinking she had misplaced the sounds and they were actually coming from next door, when she spotted the open drawer. Clara walked to the dresser; the second drawer down was open revealing some blankets and linen. Poking out from beneath a knitted violet blanket was the corner of a white slip of paper. Clara stared at it a moment, then reached in and pulled it out.

It was in fact a bundle of papers and the top sheet declared that it was the memoirs of Miss Edith Sampford, former suffragette. Clara felt her breath catch in her throat. The memoirs Miss Sampford had mentioned! Clara had almost forgotten about them in the chaos.

Clara turned the papers over in her hands, skimming through carefully typed pages concerning rallies, meetings and Miss Sampford's political beliefs. There were some pithy descriptions of other suffragettes and former MPs. Miss Sampford had spared no-one the scathing might of her pen, though she interlaced criticism with praise where it was due. Clara found herself absorbed in the writing, flicking through what proved to be nearly 500 pages of material.

Then, as if her hand had been guided to it, she found herself on page 385 reading a sentence that began "That night we planned our deadliest attack..." Clara skimmed the page. There it all was, the confession that Miss Sampford had never given in life. Though the names of the other participants had been scrupulously concealed, Miss Sampford was brutally honest about her own work that night. "The screams from the Edgbarton house told me I had made a dreadful error..."

Clara realised she had gasped aloud. To see what she had suspected in black and white... What should she do? Miss Sampford had always intended for her memoirs to be published and presumably she had included this confession on purpose, but what would the Sampfords say? Clara should really leave the papers to the executors of Miss Sampford's will, but that happened to be her brother Edward and his wife. What were the chances they would not read this manuscript and carefully tamper with it? Or worse burn the whole thing to save scandal? Clara couldn't allow that to happen. Miss Sampford had written this so others would know what it was like to be a suffragette, the good and the bad. It could not be consigned to the fire. She would not be able to do anything with it for the moment, but maybe in the years to come, when the older Sampfords were not around, she could see about getting it published? Clara knew her mind was made up.

She wedged the papers in her handbag and left the room. She hurried downstairs, more upset than she cared to admit to herself. In the hall she heard the footsteps again, walking along the second floor. She didn't even look back. The ghosts of Berkeley Square could take care of themselves, she had had enough of them.

On the way to the train station she dropped the house key to the solicitor. Then she was hastening to get home, back to Brighton, and far away from the madness of London. Clara resolved that this was the first and last time she ever investigated a case over Christmas. Well, unless someone desperately needed her help, of course.

Printed in Great Britain
by Amazon.co.uk, Ltd.,
Marston Gate.